# A Thing of Rags and Patches

# A Thing of Rags and Patches

A Thing of Rags and Patches

Cover Art and design by Kimi Owens

Back cover photo by Dawn Ramsey

ISBN 13: 978-1-885865-33-5

*For Ken, who knows why.*

# Contents

# In September

In September, the Oracle of Delphi came, carrying a box of brightly colored chalk.

Young, she came, and fresh; not yet a woman blooded, though veiled as a woman goes, her hair shrouded, her face in muslin shadow and her frame as slight and slender as any boy's. She was clearly not old enough to walk alone the long road down the mountain. Yet alone she had come, past where Chaeronea's walls dipped their heels in the silver Copais, and neither a priest nor acolyte nor even a servant trailed along in her determined wake.

She found the fisherman more or less where she had expected him and offered the poor man more gold than his family together had ever seen if only he would row her out upon the lake. Out to the bald-crowned thrust of granite that marred the water's face like a curse on festival day.

He stood a moment and considered her offer; perhaps scenting the midnight breath of Hades' gate clinging to her gown, or hearing the echo of cold Python's grave in her too-old voice. She thought, *'He will tell me now that the rock is called Mormo's Nest, and warn that the Child Biter lurks there, where roads older than the deluge once crossed and made the place sacred to Hecate.'* And she prepared to pad her offer of gold with a certain song the Goddess Themis crooned to bring the ocean eels all thronging silver to her side. A simple tune, any peasant could learn to sing it and nevermore fear for lean seasons on Copais' muddy shores.

But he only turned, regarded the lurching stone with something like sympathy. "And what does Phoebus want with our poor old shadow then?" he asked, and stepped an oar from its lock to steady the boat so she might come on. He did not row off when she settled herself into his stern, but instead peered into her little box as if he thought to find a gorgon's head hid among the neat-rolled wands of brightness. "What has she done to Him or His, our monster?"

The Pythia idly dusted the tip of one finger with chalk as tawny as Chimaeras' fur, then stroked another, Gorgon bronze with the next finger on. "The Midnight Lady's servants do as she bids them, of course. The Mormo is no different to the rest. But I wonder you do not fear this one, living so close upon your homes as she does?"

He huffed a chuckle, and set his oars to the water. "Children fear the Biter, of course," he answered after a few strokes, "but it's good they fear something, or else they would grow wild and cruel. The Mormo cools their fire, teaches them their place in the world. Better humility be learnt at home than abroad in the world, where there are Gods to offend and doom or shame to bring back on one's heels." He tacked abruptly around something unseen, submerged. She could not see the obstruction, but their avoidance curved them away from the granite spar rather quicker than a land-born girl might expect.

She tipped another finger with blue, as bright as a Roc's wing, and smiled beneath her veil. "Do you know what God comes to Parnassus when Apollo leaves it in the winter months?"

The fisherman shivered. Most men would, who had heard of the Maenads and the wild, fierce, half-mad God they worshipped. "The Lord Dionysus," he said, and the little boat swerved back again.

She dipped the last little finger into green, bright as hundred-headed Ladon, and she nodded. "Just so. And do you think the Wild God and his horde would be entertained by the Muses' dignified songs? With epic, with lyric, or histories of valiant kings, and honour to the stately Gods of high Olympos? Do you suppose Comic Thalia has endless patience for fart jokes, or Melpomene for drunken raunch when she tells of heartbreaking loss?" She shook her head, reached into the box with her left hand, and tickled up the scarlet of a Harpy's belly, rusty red of dragon's teeth grown dry and angry in earth, umber like the flank of a dog with three snarling heads.

"No, the Maenads and their lord hunger for darker stuff, and if they cannot have terror, fury, madness and blood in their nightly revels, then they will run wild on Parnassus' flanks and create it afresh." Indigo, rich and cold as Cetus' poisoned fins filled up the whorls of her fingertip, and she tsked a laugh. "Bored Maenads bring nobody any good."

"Too right, they don't," The Fisherman grumbled as they came along the island's ragged knees. All the while, though, his wary eye watched her fingers, stained, slender, and sinister in the bright autumn sunlight. She had his full attention as she selected her final hue -- plain white, like bones gnawed clean in secret, sacred spaces.

This, she held up to his gaze, as a robber might show a sword, or a King his casual order of death. "Phoebus intends no harm to your Monster, good man of Chaeronea, he simply wishes me to... borrow her awhile."

He swallowed, rebuffed the rocks with an oar, but did not shift his gaze from her palette. "Borrow her?"

"Just so. And tell me then; until the Sun God returns from Hyperborea in the spring, which monster shall I leave here behind as collateral?"

# Am Buachaille Ban

"You do not sing anymore."

The voice came out of the darkness behind her, and Brighid couldn't suppress a startled jump. The bit of agate she had been polishing clattered onto the table as she spun in her chair. "Sister," she breathed, knotting the sandy rag around her fingers as she waited for her heart to slow down. "It's late for a visit-"

"Late is the only time I may come to visit you without that *Man* sending his spies to glower and carry tales, and you well know it!" Morrighan strode into the room, the low, banked light of the fire etching her features into angry lines. She stopped outside the range of Brighid's lone candle. "He keeps you alone, sister. Don't think I haven't seen."

Brighid carefully smoothed the polishing cloth on the table. "I have my maidens-"

"Where?"

She looked up, startled at the harsh question. Morrighan merely waved an arm around the room -- elegant, well appointed, and empty. No evidence of Brighid's nineteen attendants could be seen; no stray spindle or hook, no fiddle or drum waiting in a corner, no bauble or ribbon left behind, not so much as a spare cushion on the floor. Brighid looked down again. "He says they are of low state, and should not grow too familiar with me." And oh, but the words were bitter in her throat. Just as bitter as the scorn that flashed in her sister's eyes. "Breas is the King, Sister," she snapped, standing. "So named by all our kindred when your own husband fell maimed in battle and gave up the crown. I do as he wishes, no differently than do the rest of our kind."

"Yes," Morrighan hissed, crowding Brighid backward against the table, "we do as he says, don't we? Our free men work like thralls for him, our strengths are stripped away, and our pride arse-buggered by this halfblood bastard, and you take it worst of any-" she let the sentence end in the ringing slap Brighid lashed across her face, but when she turned her head back, she was smiling. "Oh. There you are, Sister. I'd wondered where you had gone."

Furious beyond measure, Brighid shoved her sister back, and then back again. "Do NOT speak so to me! You had your time as Queen, and it was not my doing that took your husband's arm and his crown! The whole of DeDanaan cast their lots for my husband to succeed Nuadha when he was maimed, and now they've got the King they asked for, and he has me for Queen, and if you miss your rank so much, take it up with the Formori, not with me!"

"He has you for thrall, Brighid!" Morrighan roared back in her face, black eyes blazing, cheeks bright with blood, "You are bent double under his pride and envy," her hand shot out, caught Brighid's chin in a fierce grip and used the hold to drag her close. Brighid ground her teeth, feeling the bruise spread proudly underneath those fingers, where Breas took care never to leave a stain. She found herself oddly uncaring, now, that her sister's finger-marks would show. Morrighan threaded her other hand, gentle as a feather, into the loosened curls at Brighid's temple, carding the fiery strands with reverence and disgust. "He has made you pretty and fine and silent, and useless!"

Brighid gasped and stumbled at the sudden shove. Morrighan was snarling when she righted herself, though tears stood in her grey eyes. "Danu's blood, Brigh, even our father, toiling like a mule and starving under Breas' bloody reign does not enrage me so much as this surrender from you!"

Brighid touched her bruised jaw with one trembling finger. "I told them he was too proud," she said, turning to stare into the banked and sullen coals. "But the Ladies of the Danaan thought him fine, and gallant, and strong, and they all would have him rule. And the Lords thought him brave and bold, and imagined the blood of the Formori in him could bring us their strength... They thought he would be a good King."

11

"Well, he was, for a little while," Morrighan agreed, coming close behind her sister, sliding her hands gently over the taut, fearful shoulders in wordless apology. "He was fine and he was beautiful, and he has proved hollow and false as a bog track under moonlight." Softly spoken, gently said, and reeking of truth. Brighid shivered to hear her sister's voice. "He will drown us all under his vanity, dearest," Morrighan twined their fingers together, wrapped their arms over Brighid's breast in a tightly protective embrace, "I have seen it, in the smoke of the battle fires, in the birds across the moon. I have seen our downfall, Brighid, the proud DeDanaan ground under the Formori's heels, and *you are the first of us to fall.*"

Brighid caught her breath, and told herself it was not a sob. Morrighan's lips brushed her ear, merciless and gentle. "You are drowning already."

"I am not. I want for nothing-"

"Liar."

"How dare-" Brighid struggled, but Morrighan had always been the stronger, the better fighter. She could not wrench her hands away, or break her sister's hold.

"How dare you, TruthKeeper?" Morrighan gave her a shake, jostling her a step closer to the sleeping, seething hearth. "How dare you say you want for nothing while you sit here making *jewelry*" her voice dripped disgust. "Baubles that mean nothing to history, nothing to DeDanaan's greatness, while that Man has put another man into *your Forge*, and calls him 'Master Smith'."

"Goibhnu is skilled in his own right," Brighid protested.

Morrighan gave her another shake. "Then he should have a forge of his own, and not be set to work in your holy ground, with your flame enslaved to feed his craft!" She spun Brighid around with a jerk, and caught her shoulders in fingers like raven's claws. "You *assist* him there. As if you were his apprentice, not his Mastress, not the Daghda's cleverest daughter!"

12

"Breas says-"

Morrighan swore, whirled away two long strides to the doorway. Brighid's heart thundered fear, and her sister's name was shrill on her tongue, anything to stop her leaving. But then the warrior turned, a flash of silver soaring from her hand to thud deeply into the floor beside Brighid's feet.

"That spear has drunk the life's blood of thousands, and never shivered from a blow. It has driven Formori to the sea at Moy Tura, and it saved the life of my husband -- your King on that day," she hissed as Brighid stared down at the long, gleaming weapon. Two raven's feathers, tied to the shaft on long cords drifted down to kiss her slippered feet. "You made it, Brigh. Your hand. Your hammer. Your craft." Brighid closed her eyes against the tears as Morrighan's voice softened in memory.

"You sang at its making, Sister. I heard you naming it, teaching it, shaping its will with your voice as you shaped its metal with your skill. How can you sit in this dark place, silent and alone, and make *jewelry* now?"

"What else am I to do then?" Brighid whispered, wrapping her arms around herself, though they were not so warm as her sister's had been. "I am Breas' wife. I swore my will to his; to be his helpmate, and-"

"You are no helpmate to him," Morrighan's laugh was harsh.

Brighid soldiered on. "-And I am Eslind luige! I am the Perilous Oath, and though Breas may forswear himself, *I can do no such thing!*" A tear slipped from Brighid's control, tracking hot and slick down her cheek, and she hated it. "I would not ask you to flee a fight, sister, nor to leave a comrade in arms to the enemy's hands. You cannot ask me to do what would unmake me."

For a long moment, there was silence. Brighid looked at her hands, soft, because Breas had complained at calluses from hammer or harpstring when she touched him. White and clean, no trace of cinder or smoke. Laden with rings of gold heavier than any

13

chain. She knew how the trapped fox felt when the hounds began to dig; lost. Utterly lost.

"*Brigit Búadach, Búaid na fine, Siur Ríg nime, Nár in duine, Eslind luige, Lethan breo.*" Morrighan's voice was low and ragged. A voice better suited to shouting across a battlefield than to carrying a tune, pure and strong to the listening ears, but the sound of it, lilting low and heavy in the darkness turned the song of worship into a spear through Brighid's heart. "*Ro-siacht noí:bnem, Mumme Goídel, Riar na n-oíged, Oíbel ecnai, Ingen Dubthaig, Duine úallach, Brigit búadach... Brigit búadach...*"

"Stop..." she begged, sliding to her knees, back against the hearthstone. The silver spear glowered at her like an accusation in the orange light. But Morrighan had no pity -- she never had, and as her booted feet appeared on either side of the spear, Brighid knew better than to hope for it.

"Remember who you are, then," the Warrior said. "Victorious Brighid, Glory of the Kindred, Heaven-King's sister, Noblest Lady, Perilous Oath, Far-flung flame..." She dropped to her knees, and Brighid felt her chin caught again, urged upward, this time with gentle fingers. There were bright, silvery tracks on Morrighan's cheeks, like a warrior's battle paint. "Forget what he has made of you, Sister," she said, and the order sounded almost like a plea. "For if you cannot find yourself, then we are all of us doomed to follow you into slavery and darkness and death."

The kiss, when it came, was soft. Gentle and moist and lingering between them, neither sure which of them had begun it, or which commanded it, or when it turned fiercely longing, or when it became a frantic embrace, hard against the hearthstones as the banked coals behind them leapt into flame once more.

The gasps were quiet, the screams silent shapes in the flickering light. Shadows of their twining limbs danced across the ceiling, limned in gold and fierce, needy passion as War and Creation sought comfort in each other. Opposites from the moment

14

they were born, and in this brightly darkened place, so very, very similar.

"Don't forget," Morrighan gasped the order into Brighid's ear as she came, sex flooded with heat and longing, thrusting and surging like a galloping horse between her thighs. "Remember! Remember!" And Brighid couldn't stop herself falling into the command, into the friction, into the desperate, spiraling passion that burned, nearly forgotten, at her core.

It flung wide, that tightly-held spiral of flame, out of control, hungry, angry, vengeful. It flared out like a storm, and Brighid's scream as it blazed through her was *not* silent. Not silent at all.

~*~

Afterward, there was silence. Not for want of words to say as they collected themselves, nor for shyness or shame. More because all that needed saying had been said already, and both had heard it plain.

Brighid wrapped her sister's black cloak over her strong shoulders, trailing gentle fingers along the strong line of the Warrior's throat as she fastened the clasps. Morrighan smiled, caught the fingers, and kissed them, then bit gently at her thumb, making Brighid chuckle.

"Nuadha?" Brighid asked, turning to collect her own gown.

"No better," Morrighan shook her head. "He raves in fever, while Dianecht and his son Miacht fight over who better can cure him. They will kill one another before either of those 'healers' does a thing to help my husband. Midhir will come for him soon." Brighid looked away as her sister's voice cracked under the Death Prince's name.

"He was a good man," she said, soft with memory, "a good King."

"He will be again."

Brighid looked up at that. "You... you have a plan," she accused hopefully.

Morrighan gave a little cackle, but shook her head. "A plan? No. I have a hope, that just might grow into a plan," she trailed a finger along the slope of Brighid's cheek, sword calluses and broken nails scraping with soft familiarity. A sleepy raven grumbled outside the door, and Morrighan looked to it with sharp, dark eyes.

"I will leave you now," she said, and her voice was hard and cold. "The drinking is done in the King's Hall, and your Fair Haired King will grace these rooms soon."

Brighid nodded, trying not to bend as the weight of her lot settled once more across her shoulders. "Yes. You should go..." She bend, plucked Morrighan's spear up from the floor, but her Sister stopped her, curling a hand over Brighid's on the rowan-wood haft.

"Keep it," Morrighan said, "Teach it to sing another song." And with that, she was away, leaving her prize, her treasure, the spear with which she had defended her lord and her husband at Moy Tura, cradled there in Brighid's suddenly chilled hands.

She regarded it with a smile of fond memory. The long, sleek lines were sweet to her pride, the ghostly curl of knotted spells within the bright, silvery metal, shimmering with courage and surety. It had been fine work. It had been her work.

And now it gleamed back at her, facing the forge once more, facing change that could -- that would unmake it, and give it a future it could not now imagine. Edgeless, haftless, yet mightier than any spear could be... It merely awaited her will, her hand, her voice. In a way, she awaited it herself.

"*Och, ochan a righ, Gura tinn an galair an gradh,*" she sang the first words that came to her. Words for the man she had once loved no less than the sun, words for the man who would never again be the light of her world, no matter his beauty. Words for the cruel hope with which he had brought her low, for if this hope of her sister's would be, then first let them all know the cost of it in sorrow.

"*Chan eil neach air am bi nach saoil gura seach dainn gach la...*" In her hands, the steel softened, flowed with grief and regret, curling around her fingers, palm, and wrist like a falconing glove. "*Gunn bhrist e mo chridh, 's gun sgaoil e cuislean mo shlaint... Bhith 'g amharc ad dheidh, a gheug a'bhrollaich, Ghil bhain... Ghil bhain ...Ghil bhain...*"

As to her bidding, white crystals bloomed across the gleaming metal, like pale bloosoms, or teardrops.

"Och, woman stop your moaning," a harsh voice cut through her spell, clattering with heavy feet upon the boards as Breas the King came through the door. He slung his rich cloak across her table, and didn't look up to see his wife hide her left arm in her sleeve. "I'm tired, and I'll not have your noise keeping me from my sleep."

"No, my Husband," she answered as he passed her on his way to her soft, warm bed. "Of course not." He didn't turn, didn't note the odd ring to her voice, or the light she knew must be standing plain in her eyes.

He didn't see her. She wondered if he ever had done.

Reaching inside her sleeve, Brighid caressed the silver arm gently, secretly, teaching it this pain as well. She would raise no hand against him... but another, stronger man surely would. In her Forge, Brighid could feel the fires leap up, eager as red-eared hounds at their mistress' tread. Goibhnu the Smith would not wake, she knew -- not this night. This Making would go unseen, unheeded until it was far, far too late to be stopped.

"Sleep well, *am buachaille ban,*" she murmured to the rising snores behind her, and then she turned for the door.

17

The Morrighan's listing of Brighid's titles are translated from the Red Branch;

Victorious Brigit,
Glory of kindred,
Heaven-King's sister,
Noble person,
Perilous oath*,
Far-flung flame.
She has reached holy Heaven,
Gaeldom's foster-mother,
Support of strangers,
Spark of wisdom,
Daughter of Dubthach,
High-minded lady,
Victorious Brigit,
The living one of life.

The song Brighid sings is *Am Buachaille Ban*, or, My Fair Haired Boy

Alas and alack
What a deadly sickness is love
There is none who suffers it
But feels every day is a week
It has broken my heart
And sapped the springs of my health
To keep gazing after you
Youth of the fair white bosom...

# The Benediction of Saint Anguish

Saint Anguish came and sat on the corner of my bed
That final night, when I could not breathe for thinking
And want of sleep wound tight around my throat,
So tight I could feel the promise of all my future slumbers
Sizzling away in fiercely cold light of waiting to see
How many more shoes there were to drop.

I don't remember what she wore; it could have been
A miniskirt, a nightgown, a burqua, jeans and tee,
Barefoot, running shoes, stripper heels, flip flops, combat boots
Or glass slippers, I could not really tell,
For her step was quiet, furtive, dark as shameful secrets
One knows one ought not to be ashamed of, and her face,
Her eyes, transfixed me.
I did not want to ask what hand had raised the orbital flesh
In a welter of florid rose and aubergine so tight the blue
Of innocent skies could only squint, though kindly, through the
gloom.

Did she smile? I couldn't tell; it looked painful that she might try,
And I, tired, sick of smiles, rather hoped she'd spare us both
The cracking of her crusted lip.
I could not ask, though from deep beneath my pain
I wondered who had martyred her, and how, and why
I knew the prayer she would give in answer;
*The Lord is my Shepherd, I shall not whine.*
*He maketh me to lie down when I have been clumsy*
*And fallen on the stairs again, or put my own face into still waters*
*Until I could not breathe at all.*
*Yea, though I stumble in the valley of the shadow of his rod and his*
*staff,*

*I shall not flinch, for his is the power and the fury*
*Forever and ever…*


Her stigmata told the story though; Holy sigils of right cross,
Backhand, arm-twist and hair-snatch illuminated the passion play
And threw her patient suffering into feeble relief.
Another, lighter night, I might have been inspired
But I was furious with shame, spitting, septic with a rage
That hymns with verses like mine, like Hers,
Always seemed to end up at that same refrain
And let us seek what harmony we may,
The unresolving dissonance leers out of the sustain.
And here sat Saint Anguish, Our Lady of the Stolen Peace,
And patroness of those caught fast twixt Deep and Devil,
Humming the tune under her breath
Where I in my Profundis could just hear,
And cradling her hands just so at her lap,
As though she'd smuggled in the simple answers there.
As though the simple answers could be truths
I had not yet, in a hundred sleepless nights alike,
Managed to consider.


I told her, through my teeth, I didn't feel like singing.
Said she could take her neatly folded hands
And whatever sweet surcease she'd come to peddle;
Razors, pills, rough oakum, lead in a copper jacket,
or starvation-empty air; and shove it deeper twixt her thighs
To where the sun didn't shine, but ought to.
A sanguine tear drooled from her lips
Where possibly had hidden half a smile
Until its shelter cracked and let her ragged voice limp out.
"I know." A heckling raven's tones the sweeter,
Aves, Alleluias and Please No's all drowned

In a sacrament of fingermarks and ashes.
"I know."

And did it anger me the more that she might say the words
Those words - the same as every soul who did **not** know,
Who did not want to know, dared say in hopes that I
Who did know, would choose to keep my peace, -
In kindly ignorance, or that she might
Might very well know what serpent gnawed my roots
When whispers quieted upon my entry,
And glances tripped the wire between guilt and morbid pity?
Might know the burn of blame well meant,
Knit thick and patted down around my poor sad shoulders
By those who were sorry, so sorry to hear
I'd got what had been coming.

"You don't," A cornered snarl, a rattling tail, a flash of fang
As if this Battered Saint might fear the likes of such a strangled
wrath
As mine, "You can't!"
And then she nodded, her fingers bloomed apart
Like spider lilies' petals
Curled out around the flower's inky throat
A single stamen up thrust, black plastic chromed with silver
Tip and heel, middle bulging out enough,
And just enough that I might tell for sure
It was a pen, and not an iron nail
That pierced her hands together, pinned flesh to bones and sinew,
Dripped red edit marks along her wrist and knees.
"Then tell me."

What burnt fool's finger can resist such fire?
What bruised girl's pride could stand aside

When asked for truth, but offered such a dare?
I pinched the barrel, tugged.
She lurched beneath the force, gasped out
In pain or glory, then was stoic and was still
As that black instrument gave up its hold
Drew free as arrows from the side;
A rib dug out, recycled in one's sleep;
Or child that fights its way to birth.

The black pen slithered free.
And she was gone, Our Lady of Apologies
Patroness of those who must surely have transgressed
Some way or other.
And her stigmata has stayed with me since that night;
Bleeding out in verse what truths I know,
Spitting thorny truth into the eyes of those who would deny
(Thrice before cock's crow, or beneath the jury's eye,)
And speaking in the ancient tongue of those who have been
silenced,
Dowsing out the wounded though the bruises may not show,
And bid the world to turn and witness what the shining leave
behind
As they clamber toward the glory, jest, and riddle of mankind.

Let Saint Anguish guard their secrets, make it cozy, calm and nice
And let those who die in silence find in her some faint solace.
I can rhyme and I can scribble, I can rant and I can sing
I will roar, I will accuse, I will condemn the whole damned thing
And when the shadows close around me
And my dreams are hunted  raw,
When I can't breathe for the depression, and the words stick in my
craw
Then I will write them out

This sleek black weapon here my best ally
I'll speak truth from deepest shadow
I will not be made to lie.

# Cartomancy

I've seen you looking, Tadpole, and I figure you ain't got the stones to ask, so you might as well sit down and let's get this over with. No, don't look bashful, just pop a squat and slide that caff over here. I'm on double watch, and I could use it before we make tonight's Slip.

So it comes down to transit traditions. Skin code, like the mariners used to do back when getting between Terrestrial land masses wasn't an automated process. Chickens, pigs, swallows, stars, tritons, chains, they all meant something about where a Salt had been; what he'd seen, and survived. Every image on a sailor's skin held a chapter of his life story, and could do a man's talking if he couldn't speak for himself – tell a Captain where to write the condolence letter, or a priest what language his service ought to be in, at least.

Spacer code isn't like Mariner code, of course, but it's not too different neither. There's symbols for a first orbit, for a hundred launches, for first trip out-system, first trans-Gal. You'll see them around shipboard and dockside, and get to know them before long. Start with the Galley, cooks last the longest on any ship's list.

Marks like mine, though, you won't see on the crew. Only other one who's got 'em is the Captain, so you'd better get your staring done with me, because Captain won't have you eyeballing her.

Now these marks don't come from any dockside Inkhouse, and let me promise you, any spacer with the nerve to try and fake them would find herself sanded bloody when she woke up from her first Slip.

Because we're Leapers, the Captain and me. That's the real reason why we're flying a trans-Gal freighter, and all the command classes and Company politics be damned. When the *Semiramis* Slips, we both throw off the drugs that keep the rest of the crew down, and it's us who steers her between the Galaxies, navigating super-massives and dark mass nodes like bumpers in gravball.

We shake hands with a world most of these Spacers will never be awake to see, or return from sane if they did cheek their meds and try to take in a glimpse. Some do, you know. It ain't pretty.

Have a drink of that before you faint, Tadpole, 'cause there's more to come.

Look here; your naked eye sees one little black line along my thumb, and four more across the back of my hand, yeah? A microscope would show them different though. A medical bone scan would show different still. Because when a Leaper goes walking during the Slip, she starts to feel a pull.

Yeah, you know what I'm talking about; it's like there's something out there in the halfway-between, and it's calling to you, whispering just outside hearing, tickling your scopes with a spider's fart, and if you could just turn the vector a little, you could get a clearer read on it, maybe catch a clean scan, or even see...

And then space unkinks, slings you back into the four dimensions you came from, and you realize that you don't know where you are, or where you were, or how to get you and your shipmates home again. You're proper fucked, and you can Slip and Slip until the drives collapse into gravel, and you've stared down more yellow stars than you've got brain cells, and you'll still never be any less lost.

Stitch is our insurance against that. The only countermeasure we've found that actually works, and all the Company's gadgetry can go barking.

Stitch is a person, or what passes for a person in Slipspace. She's the one who leaves these marks - these scars - behind after she's done carving the way home into an Engineer's long bones, along the curve of her ribs, the arc of her pelvis, and the spur of each vertebrae. The sturdy strut of mandible, the tissue thin temple bone, the tiny gems inside the ear, and the candy shell of each little tooth all get scrimshaw-carved to anchor us Leapers to where we come from, so that we don't get lost trying to find where we're going.

Hell yes, it hurts. But she does the work in Slipspace, and things work different there. Pain's still pain, but it's something else too. It's something more, something deeper, higher. Something maybe we had words for back when humans thought stars were Gods, but rationality don't give it room to fit between the conjugation anymore. Hell, it barely fits into our minds at all, and then only when we're looking at it from six dimensions of separation. I can't describe it. None of us can.

Now sometimes old Stitch, she'll come and find you on shipboard. One minute you're at station and working, the next she's sliding your shankbone like a knife from its sleeve, and what are you gonna do but sit your ass down and wait for her to finish?

Other times it's like she calls you to her for it; snatches you atom by atom to wherever it is she makes her own. You won't remember if it's cold, or dry; nor what it smells like, nor a single detail of what you see when you're there, beyond that you've seen *something*.

But what you will remember is how she peels your fingers like bananas, and how pink and pale the living bone looks when she scratches your data into it. She's always finished before the Slip straightens out, and there you'll be, with a two-day ache, and a dozen brand new scar lines on your skin.

Once she starts mapping you she won't stop. Anytime you Slip, she'll be there. You can't evade her, can't fight her, can't buy her off. No other Leaper will step in once you've paid her fee, either. We've got nothing she wants anymore.

The fee? Oh, you'll want another belt of that first.

It's three of your bones – see my little finger there, shorter by a knuckle than all the rest? My left little toe's just the same. The other bone she takes is the last, littlest bone from what's left of your primate tail. She eats them like candy, staring you down with her atmos-blue eyes in her void-black face so that you'll know that she's as serious as a hull breach.

Some Leapers think that carbon skin is just the color her kind come in. Others say she's Leapt to so many places, that there's not a cell of her dermis, from tongue to toenail, that isn't stitched with someone's idea of home.

Maybe her world of origin is scribbled somewhere in that matrix, or maybe the whole damned Slipspace is where she comes from. Maybe she's the Bouncer making sure we don't loot the silver and track mud on the carpet while we're shortcutting through her parlor.

It's all guessing though. She's never said a word to nobody, you just *know*, is all. She looks at you and you know what she wants, and if you know what's good for you, Tadpole, you give it to her and shake on your bargain.

Then she'll spend the next few years hunting down every scrap of bone inside you, and carving them with your coordinates, so that even if you lose your mind and your meat and your matter to the void, your bones will always be able to lead you back home again.

You finish off that caff now, and get on back to the hold. Geocargo always takes longer than you think to secure, and they'll need all hands to get it tight before we Slip tonight.

And Tadpole?

See you then.

# Zero Hour, 8:15

"I do not believe you." The words were mean, and mad and sorry all at once, and they were out of Chandra's mouth the instant she saw me. "You show up *here* and expect I'll just drop everything I got to do and bail your sorry ass out of whatever trouble you got into this time?" She gestured at her uniform scrubs, pink and green under her big white lab coat. "Damn it, Rese, I got *work* to do!" But for all that bluster, Chan still came out from under the hospital's drive-up entrance to meet me by my car.

"You're lookin good, Chan." Mama always did say to start with a sweet word if you're fixin to ask for sugar. "You lose some weight?"

Whoops.

"So help me, Tyrese," she began, her fist coming up under my nose. It looked smaller now than it did when we were kids, but it was probably just as hard as it used to be.

I put up my hands in surrender -- the only protective maneuver that had ever worked when my sister's blood was up. "Don't fuss, okay? I don't need money or nothing, I promise."

She still glared, but it was easier now -- like she'd remembered when we were kids too, before the army and medical school debts and jail and divorces turned us both hard and brittle. "Well, I know you didn't drive out here at two in the morning, and have me paged out of my lunch break just because you needed some sisterly advice." She snorted, folding her arms across her chest and leaning on the Monte Carlo's side like she didn't care what the road dust was going to do to her nice white jacket. "It's not like you ever took a word of advice from we when it really mattered anyhow."

Which I felt was unfair, but I didn't want to waste time trying to disprove it. Instead, I went with, "I do need your advice, Chan." She gave me a look like I'd told her I meant to become a Vegas showgirl, but I went on before she could call me a liar out loud. Again. "I can't explain it to you now. Not here. You need to see it."

She was starting to frown again. I shook my head, patted back the dry air between us. "I ain't lyin. It's just something don't make no sense to me, and you're the one who's got the brains to make sense out of it. But it won't do no good for me to tell you. You got to *see* it to understand, Chandra. Please."

She let that please hang between us for a long time, like she was savouring it. Then she sighed and leaned her head back. "My shift lasts another four hours," she said and stared up at the sky. Not many of the desert stars to count through the parking lot lights, so I figured she was most likely praying for strength. "I got no sick time left after Tambry's asthma this spring..."

Poor kid. After Afghanistan, I knew how my little niece felt, fightin' just to get a breath.

"No, after you get off work is fine," I said. "Better, in fact. Sun'll be up then, so we can see clear without lights."

That brought her around on me again, her finger like a drill sergeant's baton poking me in my weak damn chest. "So help me, Tyrese Roi Voisin, if you bring the law into my life again with this, we are through! You might be my flesh and blood, but I will *not* lose my children to your foolishness, do you hear me?"

I felt the muscle jump in my jaw, the one warning me that my temper was going. No matter how many times I said I was sorry, or tried to make it up to her, that one screw up wasn't ever going to be forgiven. It hadn't even been my fault, but I'd be paying for it on Chandra's slate until the both of us were cold and dead.

But no. Opening all that up again wouldn't get us anywhere we hadn't already gone a hundred times before, and come away with the same scars to show for it. I took a deep breath, the desert air biting cold into my ruined lungs, and let it out slow. "I ain't doing this with you now, Chandra," I said, hauling open the car door and sliding in behind the wheel. "There's an old abandoned Shell station about 20 miles past Ina on Saddleback road. I'll be there at six, and if you ain't showed up by seven, then I'll know you've made your mind up against me."

"Oh no! You are *not* layin' this on me-" she began, gearing up to scrap anyhow she could. The 'Carlo's eight cylinders roared out over her fightin' words though, and made her jump clear, like she thought I might run her down.

"Don't you worry, Missus James," I told her over the rough idle, "I wouldn't trust you with a problem that could stand to send me back to jail." I shoved the car into gear, and fixed her with a stare. "So you just come if you're gonna come, and go on home if you ain't. I'll be waiting, either way."

~*~

Arizona's one of the last places in the States where you can openly wear a sidearm on the street. Sure, you might have a very friendly officer of the law inquiring into your travel and leisure plans if you do go about with your Smith & Wesson hanging out, but just so long as you aren't trying to conceal it, or openly threatening anybody with it, you won't wind up in jail just for having it, like you would in New Orleans.

Unless you've done time as a guest of your Uncle Sam's correctional system, that is. Apparently any little conviction on a man's record is enough to make John Law seriously question his good intentions where firearms are concerned. Go figure. Not that that slows anyone down so long as there's Wal Mart, Flea Markets or Yard Sales to be found. Shotguns are as easy to find as rattlesnakes in the Sonora Desert, if a man should decide he wants one.

Which I don't. Or rather, I hadn't. After the previous night, I found myself wanting a trench broom pretty bad. But it's one thing to hit an all night Wally World for cigarettes at 4am. Askin' for a 12 gauge pump and a box of slugs at that hour is a whole different proposition, even for Tucson. And that was the very least of the reasons why I needed Chandra; she had a gun.

She'd picked it up two years back, when those freaks with Operation Salvation kidnapped four nurses and a surgeon from the ER at Northwest because they heard someone once did an abortion there. Me, I figured Chandra's job at the hospital pharmacy put her in more danger than a hypothetical dead baby and a bunch of kooks, but either way, when she asked me to find her a piece, I was only too happy to call in a favor on her behalf. Then I took her out into the desert and taught her everything the Army drilled into me about how to wear it, how to clean it, how to draw it, and how to kill someone with it if you had to. Scared as she was, my big sis would have done my Drill Instructor proud. Not only did Chandra James *have* a gun, she knew how to use it, and best of all, she wouldn't be breaking parole by carrying it, either.

Assuming she decided to show up, of course.

There was a part of me that almost hoped she wouldn't. Because then my next step would be easy. Wrong, probably, stupid almost definitely, but it wouldn't be complicated at all.

But that part of me was outweighed by the part of me that was a selfish bastard who didn't want to stand up to what was bound to be his next great fuck up all on his own. Sure, it'd hurt like hell to learn that my last living kin had given up on me just like the rest of the world, but in the long run, it might be cleaner. No, simpler. No. Well, for the best, anyhow, if she didn't come.

When the sun came creeping down the Tucson Mountains, painting the slopes pink and gold long before it showed over the desert to the East, I was making plans to go relieve a Home Depot of as much nitrogen fertilizer as I could manage. Then a smudge of dust and rust came over the prow of the hill, and put that easy, stupid answer out of reach for good.

The shameful truth? I've never been so glad to see a Camry in my life.

31

I keyed on the 'Carlo and pulled into the turnout, then gunned out onto Saddleback road just as Chan was slowing down to turn. I knew better than to give either of us a chance to speak before there was something bigger and more immediate than old grievances for us to talk about.

Whether Chan agreed or not, she didn't let the Camry's little engine keep her from catching up and sticking to my tail as I led her up into the pink-stained foothills.

~*~

"What in the name of God is this?" Chandra asked when we stopped, half an hour later.

I slammed my door -- unlocked, keys in the ignition just in case. "I'm guessing it was a traveler's motel back when it was built," I said, eyeing the squat, dust coloured building with its five chipped grey doors. "God knows why they'd build one out here in the middle of nowhere. Maybe there was supposed to be a highway up here or something. I don't know." I went around to the 'Carlo's trunk, and fetched out my big five cell maglight from under the tire iron. "Now though? Now it's a problem, is what it is." I pointed the mag at the far end from the parking lot, where the motel's low single rooms gave way to a wider footprint that spoke of living, not just of sleeping and showering. "That's the way in." Then I stopped, remembering. "You don't have none of those vinyl gloves in your car, do you?"

Her eyes narrowed, but I guess she was done asking questions for a while, because she just nodded and went around to her own trunk. She came back around snapping the purple cuffs in place -- a second pair in her hands, which she shoved at me without a word. I also noticed with more than a little relief, that she had put her pistol onto her belt unasked.

32

"All right," she said, "You got me here. Now show me what this is all about."

I had been a little worried what she would think when she saw the door of the caretaker's apartment around back, but it turns out I didn't need to worry -- Chan was too distracted to notice the crowbar marks on the splintered frame. "Is that some kind of satellite dish?" she asked, staring out across the bare dirt and weeds between the main building and the metal shed dug into the hill behind it.

I nodded. "Pretty sure it is. Military uses something like this for advanced troops when there's no real telecom system where they're going. This one's bigger though. New, too. You can still see the shine."

"And the rest of that stuff up there?"

"I don't know about all of it, Chan," I said, sorry I had to admit it. "That's part of a radar array though. Behind it's a wind meter, and I think that one there is a microphone. Those two might be special frequency antennas, and that one in the back, I think may be a telescope of some kind."

"A telescope?" She gave me a look. "I guess that'd be pretty valuable, wouldn't it?"

I ignored her jab, and pointed at the roof-eaves over our heads. White metal clips wrapped the flashing around and under, held tight with heavy screws. "This side of the motel roof is covered with brand new solar panels. Just this side though. Nothing you could see from the parking lot or the road."

That caught her attention, and like I knew she would, Chandra turned to take stock of the hotel's back side. Brand new doors, shiny under the powder coat, but not one of them showing a knob to the outside, and only two of them where the other side showed five; windows and the remaining doorways bricked down to barely more than peepholes, where they weren't replaced completely by ventilation grids; brickwork repointed, sound and sure, and looking

33

nothing like the wreck we could see from the road. At the far end of the yard, under the nearly-dry cistern that didn't clear the rooftop, squatted a waist-high plywood shack.

"Where are the dogs?"

"Don't know," I told her true. "Chains are there, collars still attached and buckled shut, but there ain't no food or water bowls over there at all. No fresh crap either, far as I can see."

She turned back to me, mad again. "Who turns dogs loose to starve way out here in the middle of nowhere?"

I shook my head, not sure where to begin with that one. Instead, I switched my flashlight on, and led the way inside the gloomy apartment. "Lights don't work," I told her, playing the beam about so she'd know where the tripping furniture was -- not that there was much to trip over. A broke down sofa with a bed pillow down one end; a coffee table with one corner propped up on books; an easy chair that looked like it'd sprout weeds if it ever got wet and put out into the light. The rest was cheap bookshelves.

The only daylight came in through the door behind us, and through the glass in the kitchen door. Near as I could tell it, the kitchen had the only window left in this whole place that looked east without plywood in the way. I went and put myself in front of the kitchen door, then handed the mag light over to Chan. "You look around," I told her, "but don't touch nothing, okay?"

"*I* didn't come here to steal, Rese," she said, but I noticed she did tuck her jacket back so it didn't hang over her gun, all the same. "What am I supposed to be looking for?"

"Just look," I said. "Look around, and tell me what you see."

There's a kind of a sigh women know how to give, makes a man feel like every single kind of a fool, and Chan dished it out good just then. "I see a boring white guy's man cave," she said, playing the beam along shelves of encyclopedias -- three different sets, all complete, near as telling. "No little boy keeps a full set of Junior Science Handbooks this nice, let alone in order..." she

34

trailed off when she got round to the next shelf down the wall. "Biology," she said after a moment. "Virology, Chemistry," each name was a light-sweep of a different shelf. "Meteorology, Pharmaco- Jesus, Rese, I have half of *these* textbooks from my senior year in school."

I nodded. "Yeah, you never did throw anything out. What's all that stuff over there?"

"Looks like diagnostic manuals. Rare diseases, epidemology... from here on up, it's all cell biology and genetics."

"And this one here?"

She peered. "Looks like engineering. Electrical, maybe. Or computers. Could be chemical engineering too, I guess. There's some on nanotech, but that could be anything these days. It's all over the map, cause it's cool right now."

Nanotechnology. I kept my breaths shallow and didn't look into the kitchen. Not yet. "What about those? No, on the shelves in front of the books, I mean."

She shrugged. "Rock collection. Lots of fossil hunters out here in the desert."

"Except they ain't rocks," I told her, nodding at the really big one on the coffee table, cracked like a bell around an empty center. "Not rocks from Earth, anyhow. Meteorites can be worth as much as gold, if you can find the right buyer."

She didn't ask how I knew, just whistled through her teeth. "And he's got... what, thirty or more just lying around here?" Then she shook it off, and gave me the look again. "Okay, so we've got a filthy rich, boring white braniac who lives way out in a converted secret hideout in the desert, probably on account of his poor social skills. It's creepy, I'll admit, but so's the two of us going through his stuff." She came up to face me, and pointed over my shoulder with the light. "What's in there, some kind of mad science lab?"

I couldn't help glancing down the long, dim hallway behind her as I shook my head. "Kitchen. We ain't going in there."

35

"Why not? We're here already."

"Because we ain't got respirators," I told her, moving aside so she could see through the glass set into a door that would have looked at home in the pastel halls of her hospital, "and I don't know what all *that* might do to us if we get it inside us."

She peered in, wary and frowning, but then laughed. "Huh. Looks to me like someone was storing up his flour in mason jars and dropped one."

"Flour ain't that colour yellow, Chan."

"Cornmeal then." She didn't sound sure, just impatient.

I caught her hand away from the door handle, and stepped in to block it again. "Not *that* yellow. I done enough KP to know what cornmeal looks like."

"Curry powder then. Or mustard."

"You'd smell it then from here."

Her glance flicked to the wire-strung glass again and I knew she was taking in the bright gold heaps on the metal island, the slashing drifts across the counters and stove heaping up in soft mounds where it poured off onto the floors, and glittering with glass shards. There was a fine golden film all over the room, like pollen two days after a rainstorm -- you could even see it clouding the glass if you thought to look. Who buys that much fuckin' curry powder if he lives all alone out in the desert, anyway?

"Well, what is it then, some new kind of drug we'll be seeing on the streets in a few weeks?"

I had to fight the urge to roll my eyes at her needling. "I don't *know*, Chan, that's the point." I took her shoulder, and turned us both to face the long hallway. The next piece of the whole tangled puzzle was just through door number one, and I knew it would have questions enough to distract Chan from the strange powder in the kitchen.

And I told myself, as I led her toward it, that it was probably just seeing the kitchen in the daylight that made it look to me like

36

there was so much more of the stuff than when I'd come and looked around last night.

~*~

The third room of the caretaker's apartment was probably once a bedroom, but whoever had carved the hallway out of the hotel rooms and bricked up the windows and doors hadn't cared much about sleeping.

Chandra stopped in the doorway and gave a low whistle. "This is one hell of a research lab, Tyrese," she said, wandering in to get a better look at the tall banks of machinery clustered along the walls. The room filled up with light the moment she crossed the threshold, but she didn't let me drag her back out.

"Leggo," she snapped, swatting my hand off her sleeve. "It's just a motion-activated switch, is all. We got those at the hospital, to save power." I let her go as ordered, but backed out into the hallway while she did her poking around. This was her kind of place, not mine.

"Looks like this was where the juice from the solar's going, huh?" Chan said, switching off the flashlight, and peering inside one of the machines from the open top. I didn't think so, but then I'd seen the rest of what was down the hallway, and she hadn't. I held my peace and let her look.

She tried the computers, grunting when each of them came up with a black screen flashing just one white line no matter what she tapped on the keyboard. "Looks like he formatted the C drives," she said, glancing into the file cabinet's empty drawers before leaning on the side of it and surveying the room with a hard eye. "So he's out here in the desert alone and cut off, with a library of textbooks, a mess in his kitchen, and a lab any hospital or university would kill to get ahold of. So just what was he researching?"

I shrugged and took the mag light back from her. "I was hoping you could tell me, Chan, you're the brains of the family."

She didn't smile, just shook her head. "Can't say just looking at the equipment, Rese. I mean I can't even tell what all of this even *does*. Some things I recognize from school, or I've seen at the hospital, but not all of it. I'd need to see his research notes to make a guess, and even then..." she shrugged. "I'm just a pharmacist. I deal with the science after it's been turned into medicine."

"You're still the best I got," I told her, nervous in the doorway. The lab looked clean, but I already had a pair of paper-thin lungs to prove just how dangerous science could be when it got off the leash.

"So what are we thinking about all this?" Chan asked, eye down to a big microscope. "You thinking he's doing some kind of dirty? Drugs, or bombs, or bio weapons or something?"

I could tell she wanted real bad for that to be all sarcasm, but she knew me too well, and I knew her too well, and neither one of us bought it. "Come on," I said, and backed down the hallway. "You'd best come see the other rooms."

She tried to keep that smirk up, make like I was funning her and she wasn't buying, but the next room down was all tile and steel, high narrow tables, and great big drains. She couldn't keep it up.

"Tyrese, those are coolers," she said, pointing out two rows of little square doors in the wall. "Those are mortuary-"

"I know." I told her, not going in. "There's a freezer next room over too. A big one. Takes up the rest of the room left from these."

"A freezer," she said, flat. "What's in it?"

"Don't know," I told her, turning my back on her and her eyebrow, "Didn't look inside. Come on."

Her squeaky hospital shoes didn't follow me down the hall, but I wasn't surprised. Chan never did like questions she couldn't answer, even if that answer didn't bring no good to anyone. I'd used to be like that too, but the army doesn't like its grunts asking any questions that don't amount to "How high, Sir?" After awhile, you stop asking them, and just make up your own mind while you're jumping.

I was in the furnace room, checking out the gas feeds on the rusty old incinerator when she caught up with me. "Tyrese, who *is* this guy?" she asked, quiet now, not so sure of things. "Who is he to you? Why are we here?"

"This thing's near as old as the building," I said, swiping spider webs out of my way so I could go around the back side, "Guess it must be hard to get one like this new without attracting attention, huh?"

Chan's lips pressed. "Tyrese."

"I don't know anybody who could get hold of something like this, not even with a big pile of 'don't ask questions' laid down in advance." I picked up a couple sheets of paper that'd drifted back between the incinerator and the wall. There were more underneath, but I couldn't reach them. "All that medical stuff back in the lab, and... that other room; Volga does that stuff all the time. Craw and Hernandez too, if you paid them enough. Lab equipment's easy."

"Ty-"

"Only, if someone like that sells a bunch of machinery for cash, then they expect to be seeing some new dope on the streets before long. No new product, and after awhile people start to wonder. And start to want some insurance you ain't working a sting."

Chandra braced her arms over her chest and snorted. "So one of your criminal friends told you to come out here and case the place?"

"Nobody sent me, Chan."

"Oh, so you just took a notion to drive out here and-"

"I'd be living a lot better if I was on anybody like that's payroll," I bit back, and shoved the big iron door out of my way.

Its handle was the only shiny part of it. "It was a friend of mine who came out."

"A friend of yours?"

"They do still let you have those, even if you've been in jail," I replied, climbing at last out of the incinerator's shadow. She had the grace to look shamed, at least. "Ray told me about this place last Sunday. Bragged that he was getting paid just to run a case on it, and he'd square with me once he was back. Then three days go by, and his girl comes asking did I see him, or know where he's got to. Well, I knew where he'd got to, so..."

"So did you find him when you came out here and broke in yourself?" she asked, scared, but with her mad coming back on because she didn't know nothing else to do with it.

I dug a hand into the incinerator's maw, and dragged out a fist full of silky dust, floating ash, and gravel. "I can't exactly tell, Chandra," I said as the stuff poured, slithered, and rattled through my fingers. I told myself it wasn't teeth that felt so jagged slipping past my knuckles to thud into the thick bed of ashes.

"Jesus, Rese," she shut her eyes, turned her head to breathe. "This ain't right! We got no business being here. I'm going-"

"Not yet," I said, wiping my hand on a stained towel by the gas feed gague. "You ain't seen the important part yet."

She took another breath to fuss, but stopped when I picked up the fire axe I'd found behind the furnace. "What d'you want that for?" She asked in a voice that made me glad I'd wiped the axe clean before bringing it out. She didn't back away from me, but it was plain she wanted to.

"Makes me feel better, having it," I told her, and propped it, lumberjack style on my shoulder. "Less you wanna let me borrow your .32..." She scowled, and I fetched out a grin. "Yeah, that's what I thought."

"My hand to God, Tyrese Roi Voisin," she said as she followed me back out into the hallway, "if any of your no good criminal friends jumps out at me, I will shoot you and him both!"

She meant it for almost a joke, but I wasn't smiling. "You better mean that." I said, and led the way toward the dead end.

~*~

Someone had joined up the last two rooms of the motel across the end of the long hallway, but this work wasn't the same as the work outside. This was hasty, sloppy, done by someone who didn't know the first thing about masonry. Mortar drooped out between the courses, and whoever had done it hadn't bothered with a level or a plumb, but just stacked the cinderblocks up and hoped they'd stand. There wasn't a door either -- not a proper one. Instead, there was a two and a half foot square hatch up near the ceiling, blocked shut with a two by four slotted across it. There was a padlock on a gate latch drilled into the masonry to secure the bar in place too, but the lock wasn't closed. Hard to do that up from inside, I guessed.

"What's inside there?" Chan asked when I played the light over the door. I shushed her, and she flinched quiet instead of cussing me, which was proof that she was good and scared, just like me.

"He taped a note up on the hatch," I told her in a whisper as I handed over the maglite and went to right the ladder I'd kicked over earlier. Quiet, slow, careful not to let the metal scrape. "You go on up and read it."

She gave me a *look*, but I waited it out. I wasn't crazy, and maybe I wasn't smart as she was, but that didn't make me stupid. Your unit can be up to its ass in little green men with ray guns, but the first man to call 'em aliens is in for psych eval and a discharge without pension. I wasn't gonna be the one to put a name to it.

Eventually, because somewhere inside she either did trust me, or because she figured I was too cussed stubborn to give her an answer, Chandra made that noise with her teeth that meant she was gonna give me my way of things, but wanted me to know she wasn't being played. And then she went to the ladder, put her soft hospital shoes on the first rung, and stared me in the eye. "You better hold the light," she said, and when I took it, she pulled out her gun, pulled back the hammer in slow, single clicks, and went up to the hatch one-handed.

I kept the light on the paper, but watched her face as she read. Suspicion first, but that had been there all along. Soon it softened though, melted into confusion, and then alarm. Then she read the last line, and her face closed up tight as a prison door. "Oh hell no," Chan said, low and loud and mad as hell in the close darkness, and she turned on the ladder to glare down at me like the maglite wasn't even there. "You did NOT bring me here to shoot down some poor deluded-"

That's when it hit the door. A scrabbling rattle of nails on the wood that bashed the bar against its cradle and scared Chandra around with a shout that turned into a scream when the ladder went out from under her. I couldn't blame her -- I'd made just about the same sound when it happened to me -- but I did catch her rather than letting her bust her ass on the gritty floor. I held her to my chest, walked us both backward from that rattling, shuddering hatchway, and the thing that grunted and clawed behind it. One of us was shaking. I didn't want to guess who.

I didn't let her speak, didn't let her go until we were back out in that bachelor-nerd living room again, surrounded by bookshelves and space rocks, with the sunlight pounding in like a searchlight through the door. She turned in a circle when I let her go, gun in both hands as she stared around her like she hadn't seen things right the first time she was in there. It was harder to hear the thing in the back out here, but it wasn't impossible, and I watched her flinch just a little when the door gave a last rattle and then fell still.

"What's in there, Tyrese?" she asked me, eyes white all the way around, "What is in that room?"

I had to shake my head -- my chest was still too tight to speak without coughing. "Didn't look," I managed after a minute, "not after I heard it. For all I know, it's him, just like his note said."

She shook her head, shook it so her braids whipped around her face. "No. No, damn it, no, this is the real world, Rese. There ain't no Frankenstein, and there ain't no Mr. Hyde, and there ain't no zom-" She bit the word off hard, then gave me a look like a cornered dog would do. "Swear you didn't write that note. Swear you didn't get me out here for some kind of sick-"

I put up both my hands to her. "I will swear on anything you want, Chandra. Anything."

Maybe it was the hands, or maybe she realized on her own that she was still holding the gun out at the floor like someone in the room needed shooting and she just hadn't decided who yet. She clicked the hammer back down and slipped it into the holster, and I let myself relax just enough to explain.

"I showed you this because I needed to know if you'd see the same thing I saw in it when I came here last night and found it like this. And you do." She shook her head again, but I wasn't buying anymore. "You do. You don't like it, and you wish you didn't see it, but you do. The books. The meteors. That powder in the kitchen. The machines in the lab, Chan, the freezers. The goddamned incinerator!" She turned away, muttering, ready to storm off, but then we heard the hatch rattle again, and whatever was behind it groaned long and low. "The dogs, Chandra," I said into the silence after it stopped. "What happened to the dogs?"

She stared at me hard then, looking for hell in my eyes, showing mean, fighting terror in her own. Then my sister cussed, turned on her heel, and marched out the door like she had an ass

43

that needed whipping somewhere else. I followed, tired now, feeling every thud of my heart, itching in every rasp of breath that scraped past the fist of pain under my sternum. I'd have to slow down if I didn't want an attack. This was no place to run out of air, this far from help. I'd have to let her go, believing the worst of me. Again.

But instead of stomping off toward where we'd left the cars, Chandra turned down along the backside of the building, crushing weeds into the gravel underfoot. She stopped at the doghouse, but instead of stooping to look inside, she just turned back and gave me an impatient look until I brought her the maglite.

"There's got to be some kind of ventilation," she said when she took it from me. "That's a metal roof up there, and there must be some way to vent the heat and bring in fresh air. You can't lock an animal that big up in a closed room without killing it."

You could, if it wasn't an animal, or if it wasn't something that the desert sun could kill, but I kept that thought to myself and let her go look anyway. It might've been easier to talk about little green men.

When she found nothing but cinderblock all around the back end of the place, it didn't do a thing to slow her down. "It's gotta be up on the roof then," she said. "You go get that ladder from inside, and I'll get up there and take a look-"

"No."

"I'm lighter than you are, Rese, don't argue."

"I ain't arguing with that. I just ain't doin it." She pressed her lips and puffed up, but I cut her off before she could start on me. "There's no point, Chan. It don't matter what this guy did to that cell to make it hold him... or whatever he thought he was gonna need to hold in there. Point is, *he made it*! He made a holding cell on the back of his... whatever you wanna call this place. And now there's something locked up in it. Maybe it's him, or maybe it's something he made, or maybe it's something he made sick, but there's. Something. In. It." I stopped, took a breath slow, and not near as deep as I wanted to. "And I ain't letting you get up above it on that roof."

She stared at me again, and I told myself this time she was seeing something she didn't see before. "Rese, why did you bring me out here?" she said at last.

I sighed, scrubbed my face with my hand. "I told you why."

"Then tell me again, because I need to understand what I am doing here!" She swung her arms wide, the maglite just missing the wall as she turned. Scared. Mad too, but mostly just scared now. And because she was always the smart one, I just told her so.

"I needed to watch you see it," I said. "I needed to watch you see what I saw, just the same way I saw it, watch you put all the same pieces together I did, so I'd know I wasn't crazy. So I'd know that note up there was the truth, and somebody had to do it, just like he asked." I stared at her for a long moment, then told her the truest thing I'd ever said in my life. "But I did not bring you here to shoot him down. I would never ask that of you."

She swallowed, hard. "But you're gonna use my gun to shoot him, aren't you?"

She was thinking of ballistics now. And how that gun was probably not very legal, or very clean, because I'd got it for her, and didn't tell her where. She was thinking of a corpse found in the desert, and her and me in trace amounts all over the place. And she was thinking of the police at her house, blue and red lights flashing off her neighbor's windows when the uniforms banged on her door.

I shut my eyes, and fought to get another breath. Then, "There was one thing different," I told her.

She blinked, distracted just enough to glance over at the building's open door when I nodded back at it. "When I got here last night, looking for Ray, there was one thing that wasn't how you saw it today. The bar wasn't down over that hatch all the way. Everything else was the same but for that. And the smell." She

45

glanced at the blank wall, her brows down low, her eyes darting. "The blood," I added, in case she was lying to herself. "Maybe the door standing open all night aired it out. I don't know. But I do know this place smelled like blood last night, and that it was me who dropped that bar down over the door before I kicked the ladder down last night. And that's why I got to do something about it now."

"No-"

"Yes, Chandra!" She wasn't ready for me to shout at her, and I made use of her shocked silence to push on. "The people who paid Ray to come out here and look around aren't gonna leave things go at not hearing back from him. They're gonna send someone else to see where their money went, and that someone else might not bother to read the note. They'll open up that hatch to see what's inside it, and not know they got to shoot for the face to kill it. Hell, they might not even get a shot off if that thing's as fast as it sounds. And then whatever's in that room will be outside of it, and I don't know what would happen after that, but from the way this crazy fucker wrote that note, I know that I do **not** want to find out!" I let that lie a second, then pushed it home harder. "And neither do you."

She breathed in forever, just like our momma used to do when she was praying for strength. Then she managed to roll her eyes, and loosen her grip on the maglite a little. "This is crazy. You don't really believe this crap, do you, Rese?"

"I've seen crazier things turn out true," I told her, and watched her face while she remembered what I looked like when I got back from my final tour. What I sounded like in the hospital, drowning in every breath, still tasting the gas that had wrecked me no matter how much clean air the tubes pumped down my throat. No way to make words out of the nightmares that woke me every time I tried to close my eyes.

"That was just..." She couldn't say it. "This is-"

"Just more of the same. Different delivery mechanism don't make this weapon any less dangerous, and Al Quaeda's been making nerve gas in caves for twenty years or more. Just as deadly as anything we had, without any military contract funding at all." She looked sick, guilty, and ready to take a bite of that just to try and turn me away from what we both knew was really at stake. "So let's take it as truth that I do believe this thing in the room is what he said it would be. That I do believe he can spread the infection he's created to other people if he's allowed to get near them. Let's just say I do believe it. Chandra, how the hell could I walk away from this and wait for someone else to let him… it, out?"

"You pick up a phone, is how! You pick up a phone, and you call the cops!"

I scoffed. "And tell them what? There's a zombie they got to come shoot for me? Or maybe I should tell them this is a meth lab, so the cops they send in here unprepared can be the next victims?"

"Then you call the army," she insisted. "You call the CDC, and Homeland Security, and you let someone who's trained to do it come in and-"

"Come in here, box it up, study it, and refine it so it turns up on another battlefield. So it gets loose in a research base and kills the soldiers they sent to collect the sample in the first place." My voice was shaking, and I bunched up my fist hard to stop it. I hadn't told her about that. She didn't need to know that much, then or now. Nobody did.

I swallowed, tasting sour dust, and tried again. "I gave my life to this country, thinking I would do my duty and be rewarded for it. All I got was used, and a cold hard look at how this man's army is just as much about profit as any Senator or CEO. They can't be trusted with it, Chan, none of them can. This has to end here."

"It can't end here," she said, and finally, finally she sounded like she might be listening. "Rese, you can't un-know something. Even if you kill patient zero in there, torch his lab and smash up whatever won't burn, it might not be over." I closed my eyes, and heard her shoes crunching toward me over the gravel. Then she put her hand on my arm, and said, "What if it's already out, Tyrese? What if there's a patient one now, and he isn't in that room? Your friend could be exposed already, out there spreading this thing to patients five, or twenty, or a hundred. And if that's what happened, you'd have burned up all his notes, his samples, his readings. You'll have destroyed everything they'll need to figure out how to stop it."

"Or to do it better next time."

"Damn it, this isn't about politics, Tyrese!"

I shook off her arm at that, smoothed down the sleeve of my shirt, and said "Nothing isn't about politics anymore," I told her, and turned back toward the open door again. "I called you out here to help me make up my mind what I needed to do. You've done it now. You don't have to stay for the rest."

She rushed around to plant herself right in my way, fists on hips, feet out wide, and glaring. Daring me to push by her. "You ain't given me a single reason why I should go anywhere, Tryese Voisin!"

"And here I'd thought I hadn't given her a reason to stay," I answered, but she put up her hand for me to talk to, and rolled right on.

"You think you're gonna go get gas out of that generator in the shed, or bust up the feed pipe from the furnace, and then light it all up if you manage to shoot that thing in the head, don't you?" I nodded, and her eyes lit up with triumph. "All right then, assuming you don't miss, and assuming a bullet to the head will actually kill it, after the brush fires last year the fire marshalls'll be all over this place soon as the smoke gets spotted from town. They'll put it out before anything much is unrecoverable, and they'll turn what they find over to homicide, because that's what they DO when there's a dead body in a burning building out in the desert. And what are they gonna find when they do the autopsy?" She poked my sore chest with a finger, and said, "You, that's what."

"I know how to-"

"You ain't got no kind of a plan doesn't end with your sorry ass in jail for something or other, Tyrese and I will not let that fly!" she shouted. "You might be the dumbest fucker ever to break parole with a can of beer, but you are my **brother**, dammit! Mama would cuss me in heaven right now if I walked away and let you shoot yourself in the foot like this!"

I blinked at that, not sure I could possibly be hearing what I thought -- what I wanted to hear in her voice. Then I swallowed, and handed her just enough rope to either pull me up, or to hang me with if that's what she wanted. "All right then, you're so smart, suppose you tell me how we get this done?"

That stopped her for just one second, and surprise made a showing in her eyes, like she'd thought I was gonna fight her to the gristle like we used to do as kids. Then she smiled, but only just a little bit. "You're gonna go and light up that incinerator first. Turn it up as high as it can go, and just let it cook so it's ready to burn up whatever we put into it." She reached for my arm, led me along in the building's shadow, pointing to the shed next. "Then you're gonna get up there and disable all of that equipment. I don't care if you take off all the wiring, or just hit it with a crowbar, I don't want any of it to work when we leave. I'll be inside while you're doing that."

"Boxing up his research notes?" I saw where she was going now, and though I didn't like it much, I understood why she'd step that way.

"And as much of his samples as I can. So if this isn't contained, if we do need to figure out exactly what he's done here, there'll be someone in the world who has a place to start." No point arguing with that voice. Chan had got it directly from our mama, and it was just as unmovable in the second generation as the first. The message was plain; if she was gonna trust me enough to let me do this, then I was gonna have to trust her enough to let her hedge the bet. "Now I know that lab equipment's valuable, but it's too heavy and bulky to take along, so-"

"Serial numbers," I answered, then shrugged at her look. "If we're talking about things that can be traced to us, then we don't want to have anything with a serial number on it. Good chance most of this stuff was stolen at some point or other anyhow." I swear she must enjoy that frown she gives me more than anything else in the world. But if she wasn't gonna call me a dumbass again, I wasn't gonna dig for it. "So you get what you want to take into your car, and wait out there while I-"

"No." She stopped us both outside the main door, and her face had never been more serious. "This is gonna take both of us, Rese. And I'll do the shooting."

"Chan, the army might have kicked me to the curb, but it taught me how to hit a moving hostile target first. I'm the better shot. I should do it."

"Oh yeah? While you're taking the bar off the hatch with one hand, and falling off the ladder with the other? Is that when you should do it?" I hate when she does that thing with her head. She knows this, I'm pretty sure. "That thing is fast. Plus, it's either real big, or else it can jump high enough to hit that little door, and hit it hard. What chance do I got out here if it gets past you, and my gun's inside?"

"If you get in the car and have the engine running, you can-"

"Dumbass. The whole point of this is to kill that thing, not to let it out and give it something to chase straight back to a population center."

"I was gonna say you could run over it. If you use my car instead of that plastic toy you drive, you might not even bounce off."

I took it as a victory that she took a moment to think about that before shaking her head. "Nah. Too many ways that can go wrong. My idea's better."

I gave her the chin, and said, "Prove it."

Her eyes sparkled like a little girls as she told me how she meant to. She always did like being right.

~*~

So that's how we got here, I guess. Me with my lungs aching, and a dozen cuts on my arms and hands, cause busting up machines so bad they can't be fixed again ain't as easy as folks think; her with her face all sweaty and gritted up with dust from the boxes. The furnace is in a race with the sun to see which can turn this old wreck into a death trap first, and that thing in the cell has been groaning and pawing at the door nonstop for the last hour. It don't seem like it's getting tired at all, but the good Lord knows I am.

Chandra knows it too. That's why she kept the gun, I think, why she's made me take the fire axe and go down the hall while she sets her shoulders against that crooked wall to wait. I'm the bait, because she knows she'll pull that trigger when it comes out and goes for me. And she also knows I'll beat that damned thing down to pieces with this axe if it don't fall to her glazer rounds, because I will not let it have her. And she knows maybe if she wasn't right in here with me, sweating and scared in this desert madhouse, then maybe I wouldn't fight it hard enough to beat it.

She's making me care, and I know it. She's been doing that for years now, but I figure this time I'll give her her own way, and forgive her for it. Maybe she's earned it. Maybe I have too. Ain't neither one of us saying what else she might need that gun for, once the thing in the room's all taken care of, but I know both of us have thought it. And she knows I trust her to. She knows it.

51

Chandra's got the pole up in place, ready to push the bar out of the way. The thing's gone quiet behind its plywood hatch. It knows, I'm pretty sure, or it thinks it knows, what's gonna happen next. "All right," I tell her, and my voice echoes off the walls, telling the thing inside where to look once it's out. "We go in three. Two. One..."

# George and The War

What follows is a story of a man I never knew,
But who somehow laid the pattern for what I would know as true
And strong and right, and to be wished for
And of what was worth the fight,
And whose spirit I sent sailing down the river Samhain night
With a candle lit to guide him, and a sail of ocean blue
And a story built of pieces I have gleaned from those who knew.

George was a good boy, and he was a good man
Branched up out of humble and hardworking clans.
He was a deft tinker, a good man with tools,
With a mind running higher than everyday rules.
But he wasn't a rebel. He tried to be good,
Clever, strong, and upstanding, to show where he stood
In a world that was hurtful, and reckless, and cold,
Where a soul could be bought, and a life could be sold,
And but could he cleave tight to the things he knew right,
Then he might just hold fast, and stand tall.

Then the Harbor went up into flames,
And the shadow of Japanese planes
Scared the somnolent giant right up to its feet,
Sent a million Joes marching in ten thousand streets
To note their names down upon crisp paper sheets
They would offer in trade for their guns.

(And the God of his Fathers had told him not to kill.
That death is bought cheaply, and comes where it will,
But that life is a chalice which can't be refilled
Once it has been broken or spilled.)

George rose to his duty: no coward, no shirk,

Put brain, back, and belly full into the work.
He kept up the engines, the cars and the trucks,
Generators and loaders, and diggers, and luck
Brought his wheels to the beachhead -- the first in four days
With a tractor intact to dig all the men's graves
Who, in those three days prior, had charged through the tide,
Got their first tour of France in the moment they died,
Then bore blind, bloody witness wherever they fell,
To the living, who fought for that eight miles of Hell
Till the first landed backhoe that made it up whole
Scraped them out of the way and into a deep hole.
And George hoped, as the sand brushed their bodies from sight,
That they were resting better than he would that night.

(And the God of his Fathers had said how it would be.
That the righteous would survive, while the sinners could not flee,
But through dust, blood and gunsmoke, it grew hard for him to see
How the dead were less righteous than he.)

George's coil went un-shuffled, his bucket un-kicked.
He did his job well even when he felt sick
At the hell all around him in War's grisly tread.
At the nightmares that ranged very far from one's bed
To march over the hillsides in boots of both kinds,
Wreaking bloody amusements on any they'd find.
Still, the process, the pattern, the motors, the gears
Gave a part of him anchorage -- a wheel that could steer
By the schedules.  Supply times, upkeep of the fleet
Kept him sane, or sane-seeming, and up on his feet.
And yes, there were times when he fought not to run,
And times when he held fast and fired his gun.
And yes, there were lives that he shattered this way,
But I don't know those tales, for he never would say.

54

But I know he picked Jerry cans up off the roads
Where the tank-jocks had thrown them to lighten their load.
And he convoyed the diesel for Patton's advance
Through the hill towns of Belgium, and Brussels, and France.
That he once, in a village that should have been cleared,
In a mid-convoy truck with a dodgy third gear,
Watched the lead truck (his own when he'd started that drive,)
Explode into flame leaving no man alive.
And three days door to door, street to cellar they fought,
Till the column came 'round and the catchers were caught.
And I don't know how many of Ours or of Theirs
Met their ends in that village's parlors or stairs,
But I know at that battle, like all those before,
Young George left a piece of his soul on the floor --
A shred of the good boy whom once he had been,
Back when rules were straightforward, and fair play could win,
And when honor was more than an Officer's word
Sent in letters back home as the dead were interred;
Or a thin bit of brass that was stamped with a time
When the sense that God gave you was screaming to hide,
But you didn't, and only in retrospect learned
That really, you probably ought to have died;
Or a word that they say at the foot of your bed
When your arm is half-gone or you can't move your head,
Or disease and dementia wear through to the bone,
Meaning "Sorry we broke you young man, now go home."

(And the God of his Fathers said despair was a sin.
That faith must go the distance when all hope had been kicked in,
Cause it's done when He says so, and not one heartbeat before.
So you'd better keep your knees upon the floor.)

For George, the War up-ended while he worked the Maginot Line:
Clearing out traps and tripwires, defusing lurking mines
Left by soldiers, that soldiers whom after would come
In their footsteps, must creep, never daring to run.
T'was a foot put down wrong; a pliers that slipped;
A red wire instead of a blue that got snipped,
And under George went in a welter of dust,
Pain, and deafening silence, with the taste of rust
And of copper, and ends flooding over his tongue.
He must have thought sure  that his tour was all done,
But Talent and Competence are dearly bought,
And those who shape the nations considered, and thought
How useful and handy their young George had been,
And thought that a way might perhaps yet be seen
Whereby the downed soldier might useful be still:
A bit of down time, what he needed to heal,
But then higher rank, and more brass, and more pain,
More soul shards lost in gory rain,
More deaths, more killing, more despair,
More nightmares he could hardly bear,
More gas, more gears, more bombs, more bones,
More flowing fire, more flying stone.

(And the God of his Fathers had taught him to obey.
That the primal sin of humankind is looming till this day,
And the price of disobedience runs generations long,
So when you're told, you'd best just move along.)

But George lay, *de profundis* in his army medic cot,
And considered what he'd lost against what  little he had bought.
Thought of facing his reflection every day that he might live,
What he'd see inside his mirror, and just what he could forgive.
Then he handed back the letter, and in respectful tones,

Said "I don't want a field promotion Sir. You've broke me. Send me home."

(And the God of his Fathers said he'd reap what he had sown.
That the plowshares, swords, and politics would always claim their own,
And there just is no escaping from the sins of one's own hands,
No matter how your ledger's balance stands.)

George did a lifetime's sowing in the fields he knew as home,
All the seeds he hoped would grow into the truths he once had known;
Honor, truth, responsibility, fair reward for working hands,
And obedience to what his Church or Country might demand.
And the harvests of his lifetime came in flowers, fruit and grain,
And in thistles and in brambles, and in blight and grief and pain,
And in love that built a family, (half would die before his time,)
And in work to build a name that would survive the winter's rime.
To do what it was he must to greet his mirror every day,
To keep the memories down, and keep the nightmares all at bay.
George was no marble hero, and his feet were flesh, not clay;
Judgmental and sarcastic when his temper had its way,
Fell to bigotry at times, rode to rescue other days,
And last spring, he laid his life aside, got up, and walked away.
For he could no more stand tall, and he could no more hold fast,
And so he chose his ending on his own terms at the last.

Now all that I have told you, I have heard from other tongues;
Not a whisper of his telling would he share when I was young,
Nor when I grew. But once I wrote to him, and tried to make it plain
That he was my only hero, and it was against his frame
That I would measure every man who ever caught my eye.

But I've no clue what he thought; he never wrote me a reply.
I don't know if it moved him, I don't know if he cared,
For he never gave me reason to think that respect was shared,
And I can't recall a moment when he said I'd made him proud
As an adult, but I suppose he wouldn't say such things aloud.
And now I'll never hear them, though there's those who hold him dear
Who'll offer that assurance, say the words I want to hear,
And will explain his way was silence, and in subtlety he proved
Just whom he thought was worthy, just whom he really loved.
And I'll nod like I believe them, but in truth I'll never know
If I was more to George than stories of a toddler long ago,
Or if the part of him that could have written answer back to me
Lay in pieces upon battlefields far off across the sea.

(And the God of his Fathers says a lot of stupid things.
And I gave up all the blame and shame and anguish that it brings
To live by a set of rules that always serve another's needs,
Leaving mine to starve and struggle, scratch a harvest through the weeds.
I will never have his blessing, but he still has my respect;
Not overly a hero, but a man I'll not forget.)

# I Shall Ride There

Her name being Sarah, she had always known she was a princess. Sarah *meant* Princess in the desert language of the Lion's people, as Tata had told her.

"Let them see you in David's City, beloved one, and all will know you for royal blood at once." All the while the old brush stroked over and over through her dark curls and charcoal smoked in the low hearth and Ama coughed and coughed in the chimney corner. "It is warm there, my Princess. The skies are blue always, and never it snows, never. Ah, you would be so golden in that sun... so golden..."

Sarah wept according to her state when her Ama and Tata both died that winter; solemn, serene of face, and regal of mein without a single sob or grimace, only her eyes leaking slow heartbreak over her alabaster cheeks.

The King's soldiers came all in brown livery to the ghetto, and took her Grandparents bodies away with them. The men did not seem to know that they were handling the blood of kings as they put the tight-bundled bodies on the cart like luggage. Sarah forgave them all with a Princess' grace. And then she waited for the rescuing Prince that all the stories promised her must surely come.

And if she was cold in the night with no ration of coal to burn in the empty stove, then she could creep to the wall, behind which the neighbor's fire glowed, and warm herself there.

And if she was hungry, she could sweep and clean as well as any cinder girl, and earn herself a share of the scant peasant fare to be found in the walled and guarded mountain town.

And if she was lonely when Shabbat came and she had no candles to light, she might sing a bit to the rats and the moths, and recite, as Ama had taught her to do, the names of the Kings and Queens whose blood she carried inside her.

And if she was frightened when the rough men came to the ghetto for sport, well. She was a clever Princess, and brave and quick – and very very small.

Finally came the day when all the peasants were gathered together. A new Prince's men, in livery of black, silver and grey cried the town, pounding on every door and bidding the people come to the trainyard with no more than a suitcase each. Sarah did not bring a suitcase, having only her Ama's cream wool coat and a bundle of photographs to prove her pedigree. Sarah was not worried to see the new servants, proud and smart in their fine livery, for she knew how the story was to go. The Prince -- her Prince, of course, -- had called for all his people to come and to be seen at the ball.

Every eligible maiden in his kingdom was to attend, no matter how mean her state, and from amongst them he meant to select his bride, his Princess, his Queen. This was how such things were done.

And if the new Prince's guardsmen were brusque, and proud, and pushed the townsfolk in, many to each carriage, well – how were they, being hardly better than peasants themselves, to know that the skin they bruised inside her coat hid royal blood? How were they to realize that she would soon command them one and all as their queen?

She forgave the guardsmen their familiarity and allowed the townspeople to crowd her to the carriage's side, where some straw and an old coat lay pushed up against the wall. It was not a very good coat, being threadbare and brown and smelling a little of horse, but it covered her legs when she settled into the corner and its yellow star gleamed at her like a promise as she made herself small to wait.

She was good at waiting, after all – Princesses excelled at waiting. And Sarah had been waiting all her life for this Prince to rescue her from the cold, bleak winterlands. She could forgive him his tardiness, she decided, and love him forever and happily, if only his palace was someplace golden. Someplace warm as parlor curtains and a velvet settee.

Someplace where a daughter of Lions need never feel lost again.

# Guardian Angel

The morning she woke to find blood, dark and thick on her thighs, Becky knew the end had come.

The Preacher would likely kill her now she wasn't a little girl no more. He done gone on so about her being dirty, always dirty, though he scrubbed and scrubbed at her. Becky'd felt she couldn't be very clean down in the cellar with her only dress burnt on the fire and nothing but a bucket for when she needed to go. She was very, very careful never to say so though, not even to herself when the Preacher went away. Something about his mean, gray eyes made her think maybe he'd know she said it all the same, and then she'd get the lye soap, the cold water, and hard scraping brush for it -- but only after the brush's flat side put a shine on her bum for sassin'.

But the blood meant she couldn't ever be really clean, least that's what he told her, and his frightening Sunday voice made Becky believe it. When the blood came, she'd be too old to get just a clout 'round the ears for crying or asking questions; she'd be too big to get locked in the cabinet with the books and the bottles and the dead folks. He promised her that, just as cold as anything, and looking into his chilly eyes, Becky believed him.

When the blood came, he said, Becky'd have to be better than ever, do just what she was told, else she'd be no use to him, and he'd have to get rid of her. Even her frizzy hair wouldn't be no good if she couldn't behave, be silent, and be very, very good now.

Becky hadn't ever been good at being good, though. Matron always swore, hand to God and strap in her fist, that Becky was the Devil's own. Apples scrumped from Old Pendick's garden; knees skinned and dress snagged from hunting rabbits in Conley's Patch; Mickey Doyle's eye blacked and swole up tight where she fetched him a whallop on account of he called her a dirty nigger and tried to reach up under her dress; horse dung hid in a snowball and lobbed right square in Piggy Miller's face; singing the wrong words to the Sunday songs so the other girls giggled out loud; smuggling in a puppy and saying it was Alice who stole him the kitchen scraps; Becky wasn't at all a good, obedient child, and she knew it.

Good children didn't go out from the gate on their own, even if it *was* a white man that wanted help digging a stone from his mule's hoof. Good children didn't go round the cart's dark side looking for a stick to pry with, and then nobody could see from the windows when a sack got pushed down over their heads. Good children didn't get stuffed into a trunk and stole away like a piglet from market. Oh no, Becky wasn't good at all, and between the Matron and the Preacher, Becky'd had plenty of punishments to prove it.

So she figured she'd better start to praying. She didn't know what happened to grown up ladies when they were bad, but she did know that in the weeks since the Preacher snatched her up, Becky had tried her very best to be good, but got plenty of knocks anyhow. And she also knew there was worse he could do to her than just lock her in with the dead folks when she vexed him. Much, much worse.

She clenched her eyes closed and took a quiet breath. The cellar was still mousy and dusty, but now it smelled like blood and sweat too, and she couldn't stop shaking. Moving careful and slow, so the rattling chain wouldn't bring the Preacher if he was up in the house, she wiped her legs with her sleeping straw, then folded her hands under her chin.

In church, Becky knew, you closed your eyes and bowed your head when you said your prayers. It was the same when Matron came to the girls' rooms to check they'd prayed proper before taking away the lamps. But this was different, Becky knew it from the twist under her belly to the sweat itching her scalp. This wasn't the kind of praying that rhymed so babies could remember all the words; this was her last chance. And so, like any plea she offered up when she was in 'specially bad trouble, Becky turned her eyes upward and begged.

"Angel?" she whispered, "You listening? You watching me now?" She shivered as hot wind gusted through the boarded-over windows, billowing cobwebs up in the joists. "I ain't been so good, I know, but I tried. I tried so hard…" Her eyes stung and her nose filled up, but Becky bit her lip hard and blinked the tears away. Angels didn't feel sorry for you – not when they saw all the wickedness you ever did, not when they knew so many other folks had it worse than you -- like the ropes and skulls and greasy candles that fell on Becky when she got shoved into the cabinet.

Becky swallowed, took a big breath, and tried again. "I know I got to die, Angel, but I'm scared it's gonna hurt so. Preacher, he get so mean and mad when he comes round. Sometimes he looks just like them slaughterhouse cats -- like he'd eat the whole world if he could. I just know he's gonna make it hurt something awful whenever I –"

A scrape on the boards overhead. A hinge's scream. A latch's thud and click. Becky gasped, clamping her arms over her naked chest and backing into the corner. She could just barely see the door past the big cabinet, and she watched it as the boots clomped closer and closer down the stairs.

"I know I got to die sometime, Angel," she gulped out, "Only please not today! Not here! Please!"

The door unlocked, then opened. Becky's breath caught tight in her throat, and she shoved a fist against her teeth to be sure her voice stayed locked up behind it. The Preacher ducked under the doorframe, dropped his hat onto the long table, then stopped cold. He sniffed the air, and Becky closed her eyes tight.

There was a scrape of match-stink and a clack as he lit the lantern. Becky could see the glow through her eyelids as he came close, felt heat on her skin too fierce for just that one tiny flame.

Had to be though; the Preacher's eyes hadn't been nothing but cold on her, not even when he was spittin' mad.

"I'm sorry," Becky managed when the silence got too heavy. "I din't mean to-" Then she yelped and flinched as something brushed the top of her head.

"Shh," the Preacher said, and she froze. He curled his hand around her head, gentle and soft like he hadn't never touched her before. Becky looked up and forgot to breathe; he was smiling. He was looking right at her, and he was smiling, like she'd done something perfectly right. Like he was proud of her. "It's time," he said, and he patted her head, "I thought it'd never come." Then he hung the lantern up high on a chain and turned away. "You hungry?"

He hadn't ever asked her that before. Becky had to blink before she could fetch out an answer. "Yes suh." She had been hungry every day since he stole her from the Home, but she hadn't wanted to vex him by asking for more food.

He nodded, and Becky thought he'd go to his satchel by the door, maybe fetch her out some bread and a bit of cheese like always. Instead, he went to the cabinet, unlocked the chain, and brought out a little box. "Here," he said, and offered it in his palm. She hesitated, and he pushed it at her. "Go on. I've been saving it for you."

It was a tin, like the ones for comfits at the dry goods shop, but its paint was so old and scratched Becky couldn't tell what kind they had been. Her hands shook as she pried it open, then the smell of honey, almonds, and flowers rose out to meet her. The sweets didn't look as nice as they smelled though; they looked like weeds and seeds and glossy sticky glue, like the spit-out cuds of tiny little cows. Becky's belly rumbled though, and she picked one out from the rest as the Preacher got back up to his feet.

"You eat them all," he told her. "I must get things ready. Keep quiet, and you'll have something nice to drink after."

65

Then, beginning to believe the angels might have heeded her prayer, Becky put the sticky wad into her mouth and began to chew.

~*~

She was asleep when he came back for her, but not exactly asleep, because Becky could still hear plenty sharp, even if she couldn't much open her eyes, or shift herself when he unlocked the chain from her waist. She flopped like a rag baby, all loose and wobbly as he scooped her up then let her slip like a fish into a cool, sweet-smelling bath.

There was no harsh soap this time, no angry brush like to try and scrub her dark skin white. This time there was just silky water pouring over her like church smoke, and the Preacher murmuring behind her as he scooped it in his hands. Becky wondered if he was praying too, and what would he ask from the angels... but no, this wasn't his Sunday voice. This was almost like singing, only with words that didn't mean nothing, just tickled in Becky's ears like buzzing flies. She made to wave the flies away, but her hands were too soft and heavy, so she lay still until he fetched her out and told her to stand up while he dried her.

That took a lot of doing; weak and muzzy as Becky felt, even the gentlest nudge was like to topple her right down in the dirt. She didn't have mind to try and puzzle out the Preacher's droning, nor to wonder why he should pick her up gently, and not like she was nasty and filthy and made him want to spit.

He laid her out flat on a blanket so soft and smooth it felt like a cloud. Becky lolled her head over to look, but it was only flannel, common and red, spread over the long table where the Preacher usually read his big book.

Now her eyes were open, Becky couldn't puzzle out how to close them again. The cellar had gone dark, like night had come on while she was having her bath, but somehow she could still see everything clear.

Everything.

The cabinet, its doors gaping wide. Its shelves all empty.

Everything.

The cobwebs between the joists stretching and flexing like threads of sunlight on shadowy pillows.

Everything.

Motes of dust, crushed weeds, salt, chalk and ash hovering like stars in the sky above the Preacher, who dug scrapes along the hard-packed dirt and poured white fire into the grooves. Muttering, and not looking up to see how each little speck had its own glow. Muttering all the while, muttering, muttering, muttering...

Everything.

"I am come just in time..." said somebody standing in the doorway.

Had to be thin as a whisper, cause Becky could see the door right behind, and it was tight shut like always. But there he stood just the same, like he was waiting for someone to come let him in. Another someone, who couldn't be no fatter, stood behind him and stared in with wild eyes.

"You shouldn't go," that one said. "I don't like the look of him: lucky, canny, too clever. He has too many charms and trinkets, and some look potent. Too strong. It isn't safe."

"It isn't meant to be safe," the first one said, and his voice filled up Becky's head like thunder, so she felt the words more than heard them. "Nothing worth doing is. And this... this is worth the risk."

Becky flinched, grunted in protest as the Preacher stood up and blocked out the folks in the doorway. He'd changed his clothes. She peered, his bustling making her dizzy. His shirtsleeves and striped trousers had gone, and now he was wearing a long, heavy dressing robe, which looked awful hot in the close, funky swelter of all them candles.

The robe's big sleeves flapped like a crow as he pulled Becky's arms up over her head and caught them tight in silky black rope. He was muttering again. It made his face look like he had his Sunday voice on; stretching and flexing, temper hot in his cheeks, words spitting like froth from his angry teeth. But Becky couldn't make no sense of what he said. She decided, when he yanked her feet apart and tied each one down, that most likely he wasn't talking to her at all. So when he went flapping around the other side of the table, Becky didn't bother watching.

There was more folk in the doorway now. One, quite tiny, buzzed unhappily. "Must you go alone, though?"

Another took up the line. "Truly, Elder; what if his trap holds? I would not see you made slave to such a creature as this Horace Phelps."

"Peace, little brother," Thunder-voice rattled her bones again. "Think you that Hell can be bound in chains of chalk? Watch, and see what may be."

Something heavy and cold settled in the hollow of Becky's belly, distracting her. It was a metal bowl, all blue and purple and black, like silver that wanted shining up. The room was a carnival mirror in its swell. The tall, skinny Preacher turned queer, squat and round, the big black candles all over the table curved up like forest trees, with flames gathered in a blaze at the bowl's lip; the only place the silver was clean enough to shine.

The crowd in the stairway door didn't show up at all.

"Greed," said one of them in a voice like a bell or a woman's company laugh, "it makes him weak. Pride will make him careless. He's called a dozen names and a score of titles, summoning all to his side. So let us go to him. Let us *all* go."

A hungry murmur rose from the gathering, but the first voice rumbled over it. "All our host, to gather in one child of man?" The thunder sounded like it wanted to laugh. "No. He seeks a Prince of Hell, so let him have his audience. Let him make his case and see what it may win him. This matter is in hand."

Then above her, a flash of rising light drew Becky's eye, and her heart banged in her throat. Preacher had a knife in his hand -- a short, fat blade jutting from a long, knobby handle. It would have looked silly, except it was coming down at her, awful and quick, and Becky knew all at once what panic tasted like: honey and silver and tallow candles and salt and blood and sick in her throat that stopped the scream coming up.

*Please!* Becky howled in her mind as the Preacher pushed down hard on her hips to stop her thrashing, *Please no! I don' wanna die!*

"Hush now," said one of the voices, this one soft as fur and just beside her ear, "You'll be all right."

*He gon' kill me!* she cried as that horrid, ugly little knife went seeking between her legs, and drove like ice into her nethers. *Make him stop!* She couldn't hold back her scream when she felt the fat blade cut her just inside. "Please! Make him stop!"

"SHUT UP!" A fist clouted upside her head. The Preacher's words were clear now and horrible. "You're not fit to beg His favour! You're not fit to speak in His presence! You are only fit to bleed." The knife jerked, cutting her again. Preacher's breath was hot against Becky's cheek, his hand tight over her mouth. "Speak one more word, and I will cut the heart right out of you, understand me!"

Becky caught her breath, eyes clenched and watering. Then she nodded. It was all she could do, all she dared do, even when the knife jerked out of her and she felt blood trickle after. She had no tears; she had no breath; she had no voice. Her thoughts were birds, wheeling in all directions, filling her up with silent cries of *Please! Please! Please!*

Then suddenly, there was wind – such a wind, like a cyclone, or a winter storm come roaring off the lake. It scattered the bird-thoughts and froze a steam-white gasp right out of Becky. The Preacher's long sleeves flapped all around, and the pigtail ends of the black ropes whipped at Becky, but in her ears, soft and secret and warm, the voice whispered again, "Don't be scared, child." Smooth and steady, like the candle flames that were somehow still, even in the squall. "Don't be frightened. I've got you."

Something gave a roar close by; a steaming howl, like a freighter venting all its boilers. The Preacher was shouting into the storm, scolding and yelling and swinging his knife around, like to cut the wind and make it lie down quiet. Inside her, Becky could feel her heart twisting, banging against her ribs, trying to squeeze itself through. She wondered whether colored girls could faint dead away like white ladies did, or did they have to stay awake right up till they died?

Then, all of a sudden, silence. Everything stopped -- the wind, the shouting, even her heart seemed to freeze up, crushed under a huge stillness that felt like falling into a deep hole.

"I've got you," said the Angel, and Becky felt herself scooped up tight, and tugged right out of her skin. She couldn't see the Angel's face, feet, or wings -- not or even the hands that held her close, but she could feel his strength at her back, warm and solid as he lifted her right up out of the small brown body on the table.

From the shadowy ceiling, Becky saw the Preacher catch hold of her chin, and wrench it around to face the corner where she used to sleep. The straw and bucket were gone, but the chain, still bolted to the wall, now made a circle on the floor. Around it, the dirt was marked up in white shapes that hurt to look at, and studded with more of the smoky, smelly candles. Just outside the chain, the three dead skulls from the cabinet were set like pale

70

stones in a flower garden, staring in at a big whirl of dust that was fretting inside the ring.

"You see?" the Preacher hissed, "He comes!" She thought it should hurt her jaw, he squeezed so, but held up safe in the Angel's arms, she couldn't feel a thing. "To my command, He comes! Your soul has bought me the world!"

But the dust-whirl was settling down now, and it didn't look like the world to Becky. It looked like a naked man crouching inside the circle – dark skinned, but more like a Red Indian or an Arab than a colored man. His hair was long, and hung around his shoulders in glossy curls like the church ladies wore on Sunday. As he stood up, slow and unashamed, his muscles flexed and rolled in the light, and Becky's ears burned with the memory of Matron's lectures on what was proper for girls to see and what was not. But she didn't look away.

The Preacher watched too. His face was a funny color and set like he had something sour stuck in his craw, but didn't want to spit it out. He scowled at the book, set open by Becky's side, flipped back one page, then another.

Then the man in the circle laughed, and the Preacher jumped like a cat. "Not what you expected?" he asked, and waved a hand at his body. "Would hooves and scales have suited your tastes better, Horace, or did you think your Lord and Master would be white?" A sick look spread across the Preacher's face, and he closed the book as the dark man laughed again. "You did, didn't you? You invoked me in the ancient tongue of the desert wanderers, and thought I would appear to you in pink skin and yellow hair!"

The Preacher licked his lips and drew up straight. "Fallen one, you are bound, by salt, stone, blood, and bone," he said. "I charge you to surrender your true name and swear to do me no harm." From above, Becky saw him hiding the knife behind his back like a boy with a slingshot trying not to get switched for breaking a window. She was pretty sure though, from the dark man's smiling, that he knew about it.

"No," he said, and he folded his arms across his chest.

"No?" The Preacher blinked.

"You have opened Hell, little man. Did you expect no risk in such a choice?" The dark man's teeth were very, very white in the gloom.

The Preacher sputtered. "You can't just-" he took an angry step. "You have to -" The thunder laugh came again, and the Preacher straightened up, tall and shouting. "Demon, I demand you reveal your name!"

"Only to hear you butcher it?" Black curls rustled across bare shoulders. "Hardly. Some name me Hasatan; if you must address me, that will do."

And just like that, the Preacher was smiling like he'd just got the very best present ever. "Hasatan? You *are* the Adversary?" The dark man rolled his eyes, but the Preacher didn't seem to notice. "Great Prince," he said and bowed. "You do me honor."

"I do," the dark man agreed with a frown, and Becky saw him look at the table where her body was tied out. She had to gasp when she took a proper look, how skinny-small she seemed, how hollow, how fragile – like a rag baby scribbled all over in red, then forgot. She thought there should have been more blood where he'd cut her, but there was barely a shadow of darker red on the flannel there. If not for that full bowl on her belly, and the way her breathing eased the light back and forth across it, Becky would have thought she was dead.

"Now, since you have gone to some …lengths to secure Hell's attention," the dark man said and took in the room with a wave of his hand, "had you not better tell me what you mean by it?"

The Preacher looked startled, but then the gleam came back into his eyes, and made Becky glad she was up where he couldn't reach. "I have served in your name for six years, Master," he said in his great big Sunday voice, putting aside the knife so he could wave his arms. "To Your glory, have I completed the tasks of power and dominion, fearing neither-"

"Oh, I can see what you've accomplished," the dark man cut him off. "Theft." He pointed at the book, the silver bowl, the cabinet. "Rape and slavery," he nodded at Becky's body, then flicked his fingers at the skulls set to watch him, "and, of course, plenty of murder, once you found your stomach for it."

"Well..." The Preacher blinked and sweat dripped down his cheek while he thought what to say. "Dread Prince," his Sunday voice again, "I have thrown off the command-"

"Speak plainly, Horace Phelps," the thunder-voice crashed through, "like the murdering shop clerk you are. You called for Hell, and Hell has answered. Now tell me what you want."

What did he want? Becky had wondered that near every day since the Preacher brought her to the cellar, but she hadn't never dared to ask. Now, safe in the Angel's hand, she watched his eyes light up with angry hunger and was glad she hadn't.

"I want wealth," the Preacher breathed. "I want more money than I could use in my life. I want a long life, too," he added, like he'd just thought it and didn't want it forgot. "And I want power — the power to make my enemies crawl in the dirt and fear my name! I want mastery of the powers of air and fire, and the mysteries of death!" Now that he'd started, he looked fit to go on awhile. "I want to live as a king upon the throne of the world! And I want —"

"You want to become as God?" The dark man sounded like he wanted to laugh, or maybe spit. Becky shivered, imagining if the Preacher was the one got to hear folks' prayers and tell the angels what to do.

But the Preacher waved his arms like he was fanning away smoke. "No!" he shouted, "I want to be Yours! Your greatest emissary upon the face of this earth! I want to command the darkness against Your enemies, and to rule in Your name! I want…" He took a breath, his eyes shiny in the gloom. "I want to become as *you* are!"

The dark man's lips pulled back from his teeth, and Becky caught her breath. They were long and jagged like a guard dog's fangs, and they flashed when he laughed. "If only I might grant that wish, mortal man," he said it like a threat, "But no, that… blessing is beyond you, and even the least of my brethren know you unworthy." He made a claw of his hand and scraped it through the air over where the chain lay. The nails made a shrieking noise and a shower of sparks against a barrier Becky couldn't see. "Perhaps you'd like a longer prick instead? Or a conscience to replace the one you've let rot off?"

Becky would have giggled if she'd had a mouth to do it. But while she could see the room below and hear what was said, she couldn't see herself up in the air at all, just her abandoned body, lit by candles that glowed on her skin like sunlight on a kind spring day. Only it wasn't spring, it was the dog end of a long, hot, crispy-dry Chicago summer, and Becky hadn't felt sun on her for weeks, 'cept for through the window boards. Still, she imagined that yellow light must feel as gentle and warm as the Angel's touch on her soul.

"Forgive my presumption, oh Mighty Prince." The Preacher's Sunday voice was choked now, his face red under sweat shine as he turned back to pick up his knife. He moved the bowl from Becky's belly and set it between her knees. "I should make my offering before I claim rewards…" The dark man hissed, and his monstrous teeth were stark against brown skin. The Preacher faltered, then swallowed hard. "I've prepared this woman for your will. She is… is pure." He swallowed, like he'd meant to say something else, then put a hand on her belly. Becky was sure her

74

heart must have been banging as he traced the grooves between her ribs. "She is untouched. A virgin, I made sure of it right away."

*No!* But she didn't have a mouth, nor a voice to go with it. And no way to try and stop the knife coming near.

"She is pure," said the man in the chain circle, and Becky shivered as he looked straight up at her. His eyes were like a dog's too; yellow-brown and steady as stone. "Pure, and perfect, and beautiful. Any son of the sky would find her lovely."

Knife raised, the Preacher looked over. The dark man brought out his scary grin again. "Oh, I don't expect you'd think so, no; her eyes are not blue and her skin is not pink. You can barely bring yourself to admit she is a woman at all, let alone a worthy 'bride.'" He made a noise like he wanted to spit. "And this is your notion of sacrifice; you bid for the world with a thing you hold worthless?" He shook his head. "Even if I was just what you imagined, why I would deal with such a cheap, cowardly guttersnipe?"

The Preacher looked like he'd been given a whack to the ear, and to Becky's relief, he set the knife down while he worked his mouth open and closed. "But -" he said at last, "But I - There weren't any ...." His hand waved like he was looking for the right words by feel. "She just... I had to..." Then he swallowed hard and looked down. Becky didn't know if he saw how the sticky red marks sweated off her skin in the yellow glow, but he saw something that made him pause.

"I'll get another," he said, and picked up the knife. "I'll get a better one. A gift fit for-"

"You can offer no better!" The dark man punched at the air that held him back. The knuckles singed, filling the air with a smoky stink as the Preacher ducked away from the flash. "Are you stupid with evil as well as sickened with it?"

"Sickened with..."

"Fevered, mad, and blinded by it." The dark man's hand smoldered, blistered and weeping at his side. "Sacrifice is not _easy,_ Phelps. You learned that in church when you could still be made to go. It cannot be borrowed, like the strength of your bindings," he gestured at the skulls, then at Becky, "and it cannot be stolen like that helpless child! You may have braided those ropes on your altar, but every strand came from the scalp of a woman you terrorized. That was depravity, not sacrifice." Becky considered her hair – fluffy and frizzy and not silky at all, -- then shivered. The dark man laughed meanly. "How many did it take to get enough?"

"I...what? I don't know."

"You raped, scalped and killed them, but you did not keep count?"

"They weren't important, really. Only —"

"Only thirty-two women rotting in the lake, purely because you wanted their pretty black hair." He shook his head. "Even the strength that binds me here is not your own," he said and pointed at the nearest skull.

It wavered, then lifted up in the air, and Becky gasped to see a haint holding it out across the chalk line – a dead man with freckles and shaggy red hair, and blood all down his coveralls. That was his head, she guessed with a horrified shiver as the dark man took it. Two more dead men stood behind him, one colored like Becky, the other white with dark hair and angry eyes. Both were bloody from deep cuts at their necks, and both stared at the Preacher as they took up their bony heads and waited their turns.

But the Preacher didn't seem to notice them. He was watching the demon, his face pasty-pale, his knife shaking in his hand.

"It takes strength to contain evil, you know," said the demon, considering the skull. "And their strength goes far deeper than the living brawn they wore." He traced one sharp nail along the eyehole like it was something precious. "I might admire your cunning, if I didn't know you chose them for the same reason as all the rest; because you thought no one of consequence would look for them." He tsked. "You really are the worst sort of coward, aren't you?"

"My... my great work required a-" the Preacher began, but the dark man dashed the skull to the ground, where it shattered like a teacup. Becky gasped, and the Preacher did too. The red-haired haint gave a shout like he'd won a prize, and then he wasn't there at all.

"No great work was ever born of common butchery," the demon said as the colored man's haint handed his skull over next. "Any animal can kill, Horace! What sets you apart from the lowest of them?"

"Stop it! You can't just-" But that skull got busted to bits on the floor too.

"Sacrifice involves pain, loss, and suffering," said the demon, who didn't look much at all like a man anymore, with his jagged teeth, and claws, and skin like burnt, rusty steel, "Your *own* suffering, not someone else's." The nails that scraped the air were long now, hooked and scaly like a bird's claw. "You, Horace Phelps, know nothing of sacrifice, but I mean to see you learn." And he held out his hand for the last haint's bony head.

"Wait! I know what you want!" the Preacher hollered, both his hands pushed out like to stop it. The demon looked doubtful, and the Preacher went on all in a rush. "I see where I went wrong now! I can do better, listen; there are boys in the shop. They ask about things -- my books and charms and -- I can teach them, Master! I can bring more souls to Your flock! I can make Your name ring louder than every churchbell, if you'll just give-"

"No," said the demon and let the skull drop. It didn't break, but rolled till he caught it under his foot. "No, this ends tonight. Watch carefully, Horace Phelps, and see what evil hungers for."

Then suddenly the column of air was full of wings. Becky counted six of them, so ragged she could see leather and bone through the grimy, burnt feathers cramped up and smoking against the chain wall. Each wing was big as he was, and he was taller now than when he first come, and maybe if they hadn't been rotting away, they might have been coppery red, and gleamed like a new penny. The stink was something awful, like a slaughterhouse drain, or alewives washed up dead from the lake, and now when the demon held up his blackened, twisted claw, it didn't scare Becky no more. It made her want to cry.

The Preacher choked and backed away, scared. But he could only go so far.

"This is what your beloved corruption can do to a child of Heaven," the demon said, spreading his ruined wings far as he could. "We were not made for dying, but evil hungers for my kindred as it does for yours. *We* know it for the blight it is, though, its constant hunger and hatred – none of it our own, but growing and twisting within us all the same. With each breath I take of its native air, I feel the corruption deepen, pushing, picking at my control, craving the chance to infect some poor blind fool like you."

He showed all his teeth then, and his thunder voice shook whispering dust from the joists. "And from the fastness of Hell, we watch you mortals wallow in it -- spread your infection far and wide, taint everything you touch, every place you tread until even with fire and flood we despair of ever scouring your tracks clean. You glory in your addiction, strut and preen and think yourselves *powerful*." He shook his head, and then crushed the skull with his heel. "Evil does not make you mighty, Horace; it makes you sick."

The last haint leapt up, hit the Preacher full in the chest, and knocked him staggering before it disappeared. The demon laughed at him while the Preacher scrambled to pick up his kicked-over candles.

"Once we hunted men like you," he said it like he'd comment on the weather. "We ran your sort to the ground, and tore the evil from you along with your hearts." He grinned, and was horrible. The wings went away, but the dreadful stink of them hung behind. Even the sour, fatty candles didn't cover it. "It has been a long time since I've had to find a heart by touch, Horace, but I'm sure I'll remember the knack soon enough." The dirt floor give a ripple like a shivering dog, and two more candles fell over. "Shall I break open your little cage so we can begin?"

"No! I command you-" The Preacher's Sunday voice turned shrill and broke off in a screech as another candle went over and died.

"Shall I show you how to read the evil in your liver's bumps and hollows? Harupsicy is a dying art, after all."

"S-stop it!" he waved his knife at the demon and backed toward the stairway door. "Go from here, I command you! Go back whence you came, h-harming none on the- Oh God!"

"Don't run, Horace," the demon said as big crack split the floor. "I'd hate to have to chase you…"

"Enough." The girl on the table spoke in the voice of Becky's Angel, and when she did, a golden light came out her mouth and her eyes, like she had nothing but fire inside her. She looked at the door, and the Preacher dropped hold of the knob like he'd got burnt. The knife squirmed in his hand, and all at once became a snake, and him ahold of its tail. He gave a shout and threw it hard.

"What — Who are you?" the Preacher whispered as the ropes glittered around the girl's wrists and ankles, shivered, and then scattered into a thousand tiny black spiders, scrambling out of the light.

"My Father named me Sammael," she said, sitting up easy and rubbing her wrists, "and he made me Master of Evil long before mankind had the word for it. But you'd not know that name,

79

of course… Man has come to know me as Lightbringer, and that name will do as well as any."

The Preacher dropped to his knees and looked like to cry. "Lucifer," he whispered around his hands. *"Lucifer…"*

"Yes," said the girl, slipping down from the table. "You must have known it would come to this," she said, and tiny sparks drifted out between her teeth as she went to his side. "The way is prepared, Horace; it's time to go."

Then she touched his shoulder, her hand small and brown against his black nightshirt. The Preacher's face twisted up tight with disgust. Becky tried to yell a warning, but couldn't make a noise before his fist clouted upside her head and sent the girl sprawling.

Inside the circle, the demon gave a roar. The ground shook so hard the house groaned around them. But before the Preacher even got up off his knees, the white lines jumped off the floor like a whipsnare, and caught him up tight.

Becky's Angel wiped a trickle of fire from her lip and got back up. "I wish you had listened, Horace. The only reason I allowed my brother to suffer this long in your power was to buy me time. Your spell belongs to me now, and for a while, I'm afraid, so do you."

The girl licked one finger with a blazing tongue and pressed it like a sealing ring to the Preacher's forehead. He moaned and shook, and his eyes rolled crazy with panic. "Don't be afraid, child of Man," the Angel said, "In my realm we have learned ways of breaking evil's grip on mortal souls. It will take a long time, and I'm afraid you will suffer, but I promise we will not let the evil have you."

The Preacher passed out then, limp as a rag while the chalk ropes set him down soft. From the corner, the demon's voice was sulky. "I would ask to eat his heart, if I didn't know the look you would give me… Yes, that look," he sighed as the girl rubbed out a

80

few lines of the chalk pattern, and pulled the chain circle open with her foot.

"It is no longer the way, brother." Becky's Angel sounded like he was smiling, though the girl's round face was serious. "You know why."

"Men must know Evil if Good is to prevail," the demon said it like a rhyming church prayer, then added, "But they needn't like it so much."

"Small infections strengthen the health of the whole." She nodded, wound her fingers together with the demon's claw, and walked him to where the Preacher lay all in a huddle.

He stooped, and slung the man up onto his shoulder like he didn't weigh no more than a pillow. "This is no small infection, my Lord. Half this city reeks of Phelps' evil. Everything he's touched in six years' time, everywhere he's hunted, everything he's owned... how many mortals will sicken of the spreading taint before we have contained it?"

"I will stay and see what can be done," the girl said, and loosed his hand, then she nodded at the stairway door. "You are suffering, brother. It is time you took your burdens below."

The demon gave a sigh, and cracked his neck with a shrug, then he reached up to the top of the doorway, and with a ripping sound, dragged his claws through the air like it was an old curtain. Dark shapes, lit fiery hot from behind crowded close to the torn place -- the same ones that watched them before, Becky guessed with a shiver. Demons, not regular folks. And she was glad she didn't have a clear look as the demon with the wolf's teeth and the rotting wings passed the Preacher on through. Then he turned back to the girl, asking with his eyes.

Her head was already shaking. "Let me see to it, brother," she said and kissed his cheek without a care for the stink. "Go home. Rest. I will comfort you soon." Then she patted his shoulder, and he stepped through the hole in the world. The air stitched up tight behind him.

"Right then," the girl said, her hot yellow eyes sweeping over the jumbled basement, "First things first." She started to fetch things up around the room and toss them in a pile. From above, Becky was a little glad she couldn't help at all; she hadn't never wanted to touch the Preacher's things, even when he'd told her to. Now he was gone, they all seemed sticky with grime... with evil, like the demon had said. How her angel would get all that cleaned up, Becky couldn't guess.

Another wind stirred the cobwebs before she'd got much piled up though, this one gentle and sweet smelling, not spitting mad like the wind that brought the demon. Becky wasn't surprised to see the air split open again. The light that bled through this tear was snowy bright though, not red and hurt-looking. The girl with the fire inside her didn't seem surprised either, not even when another angel stepped out.

He had six wings too, but his were white like a swan's, and so was his long, curling hair, both starkly beautiful against skin like cinnamon. His sandals didn't touch the floor, and neither did his long nightdress, which was so red it made Becky's belly cramp. Even though he didn't have a burning sword like the Bible angels did, he was still a terrible sight.

"You choose risky prey this time, Lightbringer," he said as the girl went on gathering up the Preacher's things. "That was a close thing."

"Close?" She shrugged and kept working. "No. For all his ambition, Phelps was just a man. Sadly, I have seen worse."

"Horace Phelps never stood a chance," the angel said, wrinkling his nose and moving clear as she tossed a stack of books past him. "It was your ally that concerned me. You nearly lost control of him."

"I think you underestimate his loyalty, Michael."

"His loyalty?" The angel shook his head, white curls rustling against the smooth knuckles of his wings. "Never for a moment, my brother, not knowing what he... what you all have paid in the fighting of this war. Perhaps I have reason though, to question his strength a little. He seemed quite savage when you sent him away."

The girl shrugged and slipped behind the cabinet to give it a shove. "I have seen him worse," she grunted, "It is hard for us to bring flesh of our own here to earth. He did well, considering his burden," another pause while the angel inside Sissy's body heaved against the cabinet, then she went to push a different side. "I will... relieve him of what evil I can, once I have done... here..."

Becky herself hadn't ever been strong enough to shift the great, heavy cabinet. Some days she'd pushed and groaned till she thought her heart would bust, but she hadn't never budged it a bit. She found she was a bit disappointed to see that even with an angel inside her, she still couldn't make it so much as wiggle.

The other angel, Michael, gave a tsk. "You always were stubborn, Sammael. Let me do this much, at least."

"Don't touch it!" the girl cried, but when he swung his arm, the wind came back. It swirled the cabinet up like a feather, then when the angel pointed at the piled up things, it smashed right down on top.

"If you will not manifest yourself in this world, Brother," Michael said as the wind shoved all the rest – the long table, the bench and stool, and everything but the girl, the chain, and the candles into the pile, "you ought at least to choose a stronger mount."

The girl's blazing eyes crimped down in a scowl. "The day my own foot touches earth, Brother, will be the end of all earth's days. Surely you are not so eager to see the evil overwhelm me, knowing it will fall to you to stop what must then befall."

Michael's smile vanished straight away. "Forgive me, Sammael," he said, quiet and sorry. "It has been so long since I've seen your own face. I miss it. I miss you."

"It is not a face you would recognize, beloved," Becky's Angel said and shook her head. "Be glad you cannot see it. I've taken more evil into me than you can imagine; all that we wring out of the souls in Hell, all that we capture here and drag below, all that my faithful cannot contain… it comes to me, and in me it grows," her voice sounded tight and sad as she gathered up two candles and set them at the edge of the pile, where the greasy drip spilled like ink over the cloth and paper. "I think, sometimes, that I might not be as strong as He believed. But then I find that I am, because I must be. The evil cannot destroy me as it can my brethren." She shrugged and turned back to work, "I cannot allow myself to believe it might, for who in either sphere could restrain me if I ran mad of it? He fitted me to this burden, and so I must carry it."

"It seems unfair." Michael said, reaching like he wanted to pet the dark girl's head. "You should not be so very alone in this..."

"Don't say that!" the girl yelped and ducked away from his hand like it would burn her – or she would burn it. "Never say that!" She wrapped her arms tight around herself and shuddered like it hurt. "Never think it! Had I taken up the task without fear when He gave it, evil would never have found the strength to overrun this sphere. Had I understood that the weakness of men could not be amended with knowledge, evil would never have had such fertile soil to... poison..." The girl gave another hard shiver and looked a little queasy -- Becky could almost feel heat press up in her throat. "It is fitting that I bear the Master's share; the burden was meant to be mine from the start – ohhh…" She bent over suddenly, both hands at her belly.

"Brother?" Michael asked as she sicked up on the floor.

84

"It is the child," the girl said, wiping her mouth on the back of her hand. "Her body is rejecting the drugs. She will awaken soon, I think."

Then, feeling like she'd been called and had best come quick, Becky found herself drawing near the pair. The snowy angel looked straight at her, and Becky thought his ember-orange eyes were like to burn right through. Something in those eyes scared her in a way not even the Preacher or the demon's eyes had done – like he knew what right was and what wrong was, but maybe not so much about feelin' for someone who just made a mistake on account of they didn't know better.

"Too much poppy," Michael said, and Becky knew he wasn't talking to her. "The girl would be dying if not for your possession, Sammael. Surely that can be a salve to your troubled heart?"

Becky rubbed a hand under her throat, felt how her blood roared and her arm trembled.

"I have saved her body," said the angel Becky still couldn't see, "but Phelps exposed her weeks before we came and has kept her in this filth ever since. It is inevitable that she will sicken of it." And Becky did feel sick; fevered and weak and shaking like to fall down, but her angel held her up and stopped the quivering with warm arms. "Her little heart is strong though, and she is a clever girl. With luck, she will take this brush as a tonic and emerge the stronger for it."

"And if she does not?" The question came cold, and a little bit hard. "If she becomes even more a monster than the one that spawned her?"

Becky blinked at the feel of a soft hand on her cheek. Her own. "Then I will gather her to me, and I will heal her of it in the only way I know. She wakens, Michael. You should go."

"I will go then," the other angel said and bowed to her. "Strength to you, Sammael, my brother, and honor and love. Until the end." Then there was a flash, and a wind that toppled Becky from her unsteady feet. He was gone, and Becky was left alone, sprawling and sticky in the dirt, and feeling like her heart was breaking in two. Her head throbbed just as hard; all she'd just seen and heard was breaking up like river ice in spring, cracking apart, and trickling from her memory.

It was that forgetting feeling that shoved Becky over the edge. Too scared to stop herself, she began to bawl. "Angel? Angel, don't leave me all alone!"

She felt the arms again and heard that soothing voice, just a little rough now, like it wanted a cry too. "Be not afraid. I am with you. I am here. But you must go home now."

"But I can't," she wailed, although she was getting to her feet, "I don' know where I'm at! And Preacher, he burnt up my dress, and I ain't got but just the one." The Matron's face had always got so hard whenever clothes got torn too bad to mend. Becky rubbed at her arms and shivered. "Oh, she's gonna be so mad…"

"Hush, Rebecca," the Angel said again, and she found herself inching around the edges of the stacked up jumble, pressed tight to the wall, so her toes wouldn't nudge the chalk or puddling candle grease. She couldn't exactly _see_ the evil on it now, not like she could before, up in the rafters, but Becky still knew it was there, and she didn't want it on her. "Mrs. Smith will be relieved to see you," the Angel said as she scooted clear at last, "She has worried all this time, did you know?"

She hadn't known. Couldn't imagine the hard faced Matron taking notice of her for any reason but to scold, but when the Angel said it, the notion of a tearful, pillowy hug took root in Becky's belly and made her long to be away.

"Look there," the Angel said, just as Becky's gaze caught on the trainman's lantern that hung still lit beside the door. "You can reach that lantern down, can't you?" Becky had to stretch up on her toes, but she got it down without dropping it, and the Angel's voice turned proud. "Good girl. Now when you leave, go up to the kitchen. There's a gap in the boards over the door and if you mind the nails, you can climb out there."

"But..." Becky hesitated, wondering about the Preacher's things, and what would become of them, but not quite sure she ought to ask. The tin lantern warmed her knee, and she glanced at it, wondering. "But ain't this bad too? This lantern? And..." she shivered, chafing more crumbling red off her arm. "And me?"

"Not bad enough for Hell, child," the unseen voice said, and Becky found herself reaching for the door latch, a little wary until it turned out to be no hotter than everything else in the tail end of Chicago's bone-dry summer. She gave it a turn and when it clicked right open, her heart gave a leap of joy.

"Go under the fence and across the alley," Becky's Angel told her. "There you'll find a cattle shed with a pump, where you can wash up. It belongs to a woman named O'Leary, who lives in a house beside the barn. She is kind, and will help if you tell her you are lost."

Becky hesitated, doubtful despite the smell of dry weeds, night air, and escape drifting down the stairs. "A white woman?"

"She has a girl just your age. She'll not turn you away," the Angel promised. "Go on now, and see if she has an old dress to spare."

Becky wanted to run, wanted to scramble after the scent of freedom and hope and leave the Preacher's filthy basement to whatever fate her Angel had in mind. But halfway up the stairs, she had to stop, had to turn back and ask, even though she knew she hadn't any right.

"Angel? You ain't gonna leave me now, are you? Just cause you got the Preacher?" Oh, she shouldn't ask, she knew. She was going too far, and being horrid selfish, but Becky just had to know. "You'll look out for me, won't you Angel? Please?"

The silence when on so long, Becky felt sure she'd spoiled it all; that the only way she'd have her Angel again would be if she ran back down and stole the Preacher's books to learn the way to *make* him come back to her. But before she took a step downward, the voice came curling round her ear again, soft as a sigh.

"All your life, child," the Angel said, a little sadly. "I will watch you all your life."

And that was good enough for her.

# Late Fees

"A diamond."

"Yes," the girl said, hoisting the gem eagerly, "the biggest in the Queen's own jewel box. They say it came from lands where cats grow as big as bears, and hunt horses instead of mice, and that it cost the lives of a hundred slaves to wrest it from the earth. Do you want it?"

It had been so long since he had seen a girl. He'd forgot how cleverly their bits and pieces worked, until he fashioned himself a pair of hands, and set the palms down to caress the book in front of him. "Why would I want a stone filled with death?"

The girl's eyes brightened, swam with water and anguish. "Because it was the best thing I could find! It's a diamond! I nearly died getting it! Surely it's worth more than my late fees!"

"Late fees?" he murmured, more interested in how her lips shaped the words than in the words themselves. Then a slither of smoke from the furnace crept past him, bearing several twinkling stars in its coils, reminding him of the problem. "There are no fees for late returns," he intoned. "The scrolls make their way back to the library when they are wanted again. No mortal has the power to keep them any longer."

The girl blinked, then put the absurdly large diamond down onto the counter. "They don't? Then. Then the man downstairs, who said..."

"Was lying. Yes. He does this sometimes when he gets bored." Wide eyed, the girl stared around the towering stacks, clearly unsure how anyone could ever find themselves bored in such a place as this. He let himself laugh at her confusion, felt the old, strange sensation of mirth ripple through him like starry smoke. "He does not care for reading over much, but he serves to keep the idle from disturbing my studies, and he does not generally cause too much damage."

The girl flicked a glance at the diamond in her hand, and her cheeks coloured with anger or shame. Before she could stuff it into her pocket, he reached out one of his new-made hands, and plucked the stone from its chain. "Can you read, girl?"

"Course I can," she gulped, her eyes fixed to the stone that gleamed and sparkled in the long sunlight. "What d'you think I'd have wanted with the Scroll of Alderstane if I couldn't! But I thought you said there were no fees…"

"Then one may assume you also write?" he ignored her latter question, and as another curl of smoke nosed up from the netherdoor, he set the purloined gem carefully between its starry eyes. It dipped its head, genuflection or adjustment to the cold weight of it, and then whisked itself out of the windows and away to the palace.

"Yes," The girl answered with considerably less heat, as she watched him draw parchment from the rack, and pluck a reed pen and ink from the well behind him. "I write too."

"Then come sit with me. Tell me the story of how you came to steal the Queen's largest diamond, write it out in the letters you know, and we will consider that payment enough for any tardiness."

"A confession?" and her voice cracked over notions of dank cells where one might never see paper or prose again for all ones lightless years.

"No," he leaned down close, lifted his veil aside to reveal a face he'd only just remembered having once. The girl's eyes lit with amazement as he put the pen into her hand. "I'd more in mind an adventure."

# The Boy Who Is Not Harry Potter

He washes the King's Cross glass.
Long, smooth strokes, toe-tipping top to stooping bottom,
And he's good.
Hardly any streaks, and not a stray soapy drip
To stain the underground undergrime underfoot
Just like the General taught him.
And he's good.
He doesn't filch, doesn't nick, even when he's shaking hungry,
Belly knotted around the laughter of roaming chavs and tossers
Glammed up in nylon gilt to mock his working day
Slosh his water over,
Spit on the spotless pane so he'll do it twice for once's pay.

"Good men work, boy," the General says,
All rheumy blue glare and mission bin uniform;
"Good men work, and bad men steal."
And the General doesn't hold with bad men,
And so neither does he.  Even when he's cold, mad, or hungry.

Let them pinch what isn't theirs, wallets, crisps, flash shoes, or
girls' hearts;
He's never done, not even when his Dudley said he had and was
believed;
Not so much as a blanket or extra State Home shirt when he ran,
neither.
He's always worked, and hard, too
He isn't afraid of it.
And in the General's billet below the rumble,
Working hard is what makes a man good.
Makes a boy a good man;
Earns him a place at the night fire when the transit cops have gone,
And a blanket that's his to keep even if he leaves it lie.

A better name too, one that doesn't drip with loathing
Or splat his face when it's spat.
Slash, they call him, for the mark on his face,
And for how he carves soapy glass clean in seconds,
Like old Sweeny carving stubble.
Corporal Slash, now the General's fading to mumbles,
And he does the old man's windows too.
He takes his share when they parcel out the dosh
And he feeds his Officer first and choicest,
For love of the old warrior bum's blue eyes --
The first he can recall that have looked at him with pride.

If, some nights, he dreams himself
Doing battle with wizards and dragons
Instead of fingerprints and spittle;
Flying high on broomstick, gryphon, or charmed Anglia
Not dodging trains and transit cops to reach his bed;
Painting the air with magic, wand in one hand, destiny in the other;
Loving, fighting, saving the world...
Well.
He keeps it mum.
Nobody came to save him, all the wishing years;
No heavy tread on the stair, no hinge bursting door,
There were no owls to stop coming.
And so he saved himself, and left the world to other heroes.

He takes no shame in that.
Just cleans his glass, ignores the laughter,
And when his scarred face aches too much to sleep,
He jumps the trains and rides in darkness
Just as though he's flying.

# Fit to Judge

You hear a lot, these days, about what folks are doing wrong
And every two bit pundit adds a chorus to the same old song
How that one's wicked, that one's wrong, and this one's just plain sick
And not one single word on what it is that makes them tick
No single scrap of reason over just what it could be
Makes the 'wicked,' 'wrong,' and 'sick' feel that's the best path they could see.
And when the likes of me are getting sloshed with righteous wrath,
It kinda makes me want to kick your skinny, privileged ass and tell you,

You ain't fit to judge me, mister; you ain't fit to know.
You never tried to put your foot into my shoe and walk, and so
You've no idea the time it takes to get a mile along
No, you ain't fit to tell me that I'm wrong!

So you don't like my birth control, and you don't like my choice
And you bible-swear your jihad is to be the unborn's voice.
You call me slut and murderess, and filthy, lazy whore
But 'welfare queen's' your name for those with kids they can't afford!
And funny thing about it, is a rapist don't much care
About a victim's birth control, nor what he sires there.
So you can have the aspirin I won't keep between my knees
And you know where to stick it when you find my choice don't please

You ain't fit to judge me, sister; you ain't fit to bitch
You never had to see how far my paycheck has to stretch
You ain't the one who works three jobs and still can't get along
So you ain't fit to say my choosing's wrong!

So you don't like my BMI; my waistline make you sick
You sling out 'lardass,' 'slob,' 'obese,' then snigger like a prick
My attitude ain't suitable, cause I don't seem ashamed
Nor hate myself enough for the unsightliness you've named
And when I strut, or when I dance, or I laugh right in your face
You'll all but bust a vein trying to put me in 'my place'
But there's a million different factors in each metabolic play
And you look like an asshole when you claim the one true way

You ain't fit to judge me, cousin; you ain't fit to preach
Some fad you heard on Oprah don't give you the right to teach
Your self-loathing to the masses with your privilege perched on
top
No, you ain't fit to be my fitness cop!

You don't have to like my haircut, you don't have to like my jeans
You don't have to like my politics, my sex life, or my dreams.
My religion's not your business, who I love is not your say
But this Christ you claim to speak for had some words, back in the
day,
Bout camels, eyes of needles, and a miser's heaven odds,
How Faith was not for sale, and what was Caesar's was not God's
And just who would do the judging when the run of life was
through
And that book is pretty clear; the final say don't fall to you

Cause you ain't fit to judge me, neighbor; you ain't fit to throw
A single stone at folks like me, cause deep inside, you know
You and I, we ain't so different, and your sins weigh just the same
And your moral high-ground soapbox isn't worthy of the name

No, you ain't fit to judge me, but just set that gavel by

And listen when you listen, don't just plan your next reply
I bet you lunch between us we can find some common sense
Once we cut through all the bullshit
and the rhetoric and dogma
And the soundbyte blame and ugly names
and finger-pointing quagmires
And the shock jocks and the stooges
and the lobbyists and scrooges
And act as if there's more between the two of us
Alike, than difference.
But that's just my two cents.

# Singing Each to Each.

The wind howls ragged and raw and throbbing across the chimney holes that pepper this crumbling basalt. If I lean my left ear into the blast, close my eyes and hold my breath listening, I might winnow out the strange words, the rhythmic, mad tune behind the slash and boom of the tide below. And if I kneel, my right ear to the chimney hole just there where firelight claws the mist, I might hear a girl screaming through a wad of fabric tied tight between her jaws.

*I* want to scream.

I want to bellow into the building storm and the cancer it's concealing under its lacy skirts of tide and sodden rock. I want to howl and stamp and wave my flashlight in the air – "Here! They're here! Hurry up, or it'll be too-"

*Late*

I don't scream.

Because I don't want to wake my roommate. Again. I don't want to weather the sidelong looks from couple 34B, whose sleeping heads aren't quite ten feet above me. Why don't they put soundproofing between apartment floors? Why are people so damned careless?

Lightning offshore, percussive and searing as it stitches sea to sky. I count the miles in whispered seconds until the snarl rolls through, tympanic counterpoint to the scrabbling tide's retreat. It shouldn't sound like a bell, but it always does.

*Time to go now.*

I don't want to go. There's no point. He's gone, she's safe, the Christmas killings are over. No dream can change that. No dream can unmake that lucky shot.

*Time to go. Time to go.*

The stairs are clear this time, smooth and level down the cliff face, as if scooped hot out of butter. I use both hands, not trusting the storm despite three hundred sixty four nights when I've not been plucked off these stairs and smashed on the dream-rocks below. I cling like a spider all the way down to the stinking, startled tidepools, and only let go when I've both feet on the level path. It runs like a pier from the lea of the guardian stone straight into the dripping, fire lit cave the full moon, unseen behind the storm, has chivvied out of the winter sea.

*Hurry now. Hurry. You can't be late, or else...*

My dreaming mind doesn't shut up just for the telling of it. I've had a year to learn that. I'd chew my arm off and leave it behind in this dream if I thought I'd never have to go through this weed clung, dripping tunnel again, holding my breath while the slime glides beneath my boots.

*Should be barefoot, really. Shoes seem disrespectful in this...*

Fuck, it's just a cave. Just a cave the sea keeps secret, and all it leads to is a natural rock formation. Nothing hatched beneath the spires of Sentinel Cove, patient and blind and hungry. Nothing chewed the basalt into crazy switchback patterns until its teeth finally found air and water and blood

*Shut UP!*

Just a sea cave. Interesting geological formation. It's only the bizarrely low tides that show the entrance, and of course the moon and planets affect all that. Astrological coincidence and that's all. Full moon on the winter Solstice five years running is long odds, but hardly impossible. No reason an eclipse this year... the sixth year, would be strange either. Coincidence. Natural, rational explanations for all of it.

Except for the dead girls. But psychos find the stupidest things to justify what they do. Chris was no different... just... smarter. That's all.

97

*You ever hear of a skeleton key, Michaela?*
Shut up…

~*~

"You're not going in today, are you?" Stephanie asks, precisely rumpled in her panties and faded concert T. Her hair's a mess, and her eyes are hollow pits of bone. I guess she didn't sleep either.

I shake my head clear and fix my eyes back on the coffeepot. "Yeah."

"You look like hell, girl," she says, and slips past me for to fetch down her mug. I don't flinch. Go me. "Look, nobody would say anything if you just took a personal day, would they?" she asks, all sympathy and sensible concern.

The coffee pot's beep buys me time to think. Would they say anything? Not to my face, but their looks when they thought I couldn't see, their whispers once I'd left the room, their filthy speculations would be bad enough. Do they think I loved him, pathetic and hopeless in the worship of a frump for the football star? Would pathetic grief better excuse my hiding away on the anniversary of his disappearance than cold-bellied horror? Could I possibly be lucky enough that they'd stop guessing there?

I shake my head, and reach down the Splenda. I hate it, chemical tang like metal slag and dreadful in mortal combat at the back of my throat, but I haven't got the luxury of sugar like Steph does. Damned cheerleader metabolism. "I have to go in," I tell her. "The memorial vigil's next week." Christmas week, not because that's when his body turned up -- unlike his victims, Chris' body never did come to land, -- but because we all clearly don't have enough to make us feel like crap at this time of year.

But we're cops, and cops do this kind of thing. So the department will pay us half time to go waste an hour in St. Mary's

98

of the Sea, buy a bunch of candles, and wait for some sign that Detective Chris Dennis is resting in peace instead of rotting in Hell. And I'll go with them, count heartbeats and try not to remember.

Steph's looking at me, all eyebrow. About to ask 'so what', just as if she's not going to have to be there too. Miss Nayatt, fiancée of the fallen, best beloved of our lost comrade and all that crap, for all she's lived here with me since the night I saved her from him.

Will she lean on me, I wonder? Will she press close to my side so I can smell the sea on her breath, and feel her bones shivering inside the smooth, cold sleeve of her skin? Or will she pull out that drama club charm, channel the sorrowful virgin, and seduce the whole department with her gentle woe? She's done both over the past year. I can't tell which act I hate more.

She cocks her head, and I think that I hear "So what?" in her New England twang, I'll have to put the coffee cup in there sideways. "So we've all got to do psych evals now," I say quickly, "Vicarious trauma, delayed reaction. Some bullshit like that."

"Psych evals. Even for the evidence clerks?" she asks, and her eyes twinkle. There's a dimple in her right cheek, and I have to make myself look away so I won't imagine a tiny eel chewing its way through that peach-soft flesh and swimming away in blue tide. Her fingers brush mine, and this time I do flinch. "So what are you gonna tell them, Mickey?"

I shrug, and turn the cup in my hands. "The truth." And for a second, my heart trips over itself, though I can't quite tell whether it's from joy, or alarm.

She's staring at me when I glance up, eyes round and blue, face pale as chalk, pale as sand, pale as bone. She's rubbing at her wrist, where the ropes were too slick, too thick to cut without sawing. *You never left the cave,* I want to say. *You're still there, tied to that stone, waiting for the Solstice tide to let you out...*

99

But I haven't the nerve.

Then she laughs, and the sound is high and nervous. "Well you see, Doctor," she manages after a moment, "After I killed the bad guy that everyone thought was a good guy, and rescued the princess, we both took off and lived happily ever after in my castle," she waves a hand at the cheap, grimy kitchenette; laminate so weary that no amount of scrubbing can bring it near clean, appliances functioning more out of senile habit than competence. "Except for the part where we both get nightmares, you can barely go outside, I can't look a guy straight in the eye, and nobody knows that the boogieman isn't still out there killing girls every winter. Jesus, Mickey, no wonder nobody at the department gets your jokes!"

*Chris got my jokes.* I don't have the nerve to say that either.

"I'll tell them the truth," I say into the cup. "That I can't remember what happened."

The look she gives me stinks of pity. That's it. Time to leave. I gulp the coffee so fast I don't taste the Splenda through the burn. "Yeah, so. You working tonight?" So I know whether I'll have to sneak past her when I get home, and hide in my room from the smell of the sea, and her drowned, flattened a's.

"Yeah. A double. I figured I could use the distraction. Come by for dinner?" At my hesitation, she strokes her fingers down my uniform shirt, leaving no wet streaks behind. "Come on, Mickey. I need someone to keep that creep Hayden off my ass. He never hangs around for long when you're in…"

And I nod. Damn it. I do whatever she wants me to do, and I'm pathetic, and on good days I can almost pretend we don't both know it. Maybe she thinks I'm in love with her, frump for cheerleader in some alt-lifestyle after school special. Maybe.

Either way, I'll go to the Shoreline café, cockblock the department's token prick. I'll let her serve me dinner and choke it down while I pretend I can't see her bones peeking out of her flesh, and smell death and sea-wrack hiding behind her perfume.

~*~

Actually, I lied.

It's not a department wide Psych eval, just a cozy little sit down, heart to heart, date over coffee between me and Internal Affairs. Not something I can ditch, really, even if I didn't so desperately need to stay busy. With the solstice breathing down my neck, if I don't keep to some kind of pattern I'll come apart before then.

I have to pretend everything's fine. Pretend until it's true. I'm good at that.

So I'm punctual and I'm polite, and I spend my first hour at work facing an unsmiling stranger in interview room #3. Cameras running just to make it official, because it kind of is. Funny how little I care about maybe losing my job now that I may be losing my mind.

I feel sorry for the IA guy, actually. He's the automatic villain, henchman of The Man, the flinty right hand of Big Brother panting down the neck of every cop here. He hasn't got a hope of welcome no matter which department he walks into, and nothing can change that. He was probably a great guy when he took the job, before suspicion and disgust scraped all trace of kindness out of his face. Might still be a great guy on the weekends; foster stray puppies, volunteer with the homeless, man suicide hotlines... but I'm guessing that terrifyingly neutral face he's wearing has been in place so long it's gone permanent.

I wonder what his wife thinks of it.

"Officer Delaney," he says to the file in his hands. It's a thick one, so it can't be mine. Hayden's then. "Please tell me what happened on Monday."

101

I don't start the story with waking up screaming as usual, but it's a near thing. It's harder to keep the sarcasm in check when I'm tired. And I'm tired all the time these days…which is why we're here, really. I take a drink of my coffee and shrug. "Short form? We traded insults, and I won."

Finally he looks at me. "Explain "won" please."

"Rules of verbal sparring; the first one to swing has lost the argument." Damn, I can't say that without smiling. I should be trying harder. This is important. "Look, Hayden comes down to the Evidence locker anytime he's had a bad day, and he takes it out on me. It's just his way of… I don't know, maybe keeping his cool out on the street. He busts my chops a little," The IA guy eyebrows, and I hasten to add, "Figuratively that is. Then he doesn't feel like him and his mustache have as much to prove out there on the street, right? Sure, he's been worse since his partner disappeared last year, but it's usually just hot air. So I pay it no mind."

The IA guy sets his pen down and laces his fingers together. He still hasn't tasted his coffee. When did I start to notice things like that? "Maybe you should give me the long form," he says.

"We only have an hour."

He accedes the point with a nod. "I've gathered that Detective Hayden is a candidate for anger management training, so you can consider that point made. But I still need the details on Monday's altercation. Why don't you start with the notebook?"

I don't flinch, and this is mainly because I don't breathe until my heart manages to find its pace again. I knew this had to be coming. "The notebook's not relevant," I try.

"Officer Delaney, we have a Detective with a broken wrist, possibly facing a disciplinary hearing, and several witness reports to corroborate here. All statements mention that notebook. That makes it relevant."

"No, see it was just Hayden's excuse du jour, is all." He isn't buying. Shit.

"Tell me about it anyway."

"Ok, look. I do my job and I do it well, but there's a lot of downtime that goes with sitting around in the Hole waiting for someone to check a box in or out. I get bored." It suddenly occurs to me that I *am* telling him the truth, just as I'd threatened. I have to squelch the urge to giggle.

"And so you write to fill the time?"

"Case studies."

He gives me a look. "Current cases?"

And I have to nod. "Sometimes. If they're interesting. I mean, I see all the evidence lists anyway, and you know how cops gossip when you feed them. I just listen, and write down what I think is... interesting."

"And you found one of Detective Hayden's cases interesting? The Christmas Killer?" He's frowning now, and I shake my head to stop where he's about to take this.

"I don't meddle. I don't talk to witnesses, I don't break chain of evidence, or compromise case files." And that's true too. Because Chris was just helpful enough, just careless enough with his paperwork, and so I never had to. The IA guy, I'm thinking, wouldn't see it like that though. "I just..." I shrug, "watch, listen, and put together what I hear in my own way."

"All right. Then what?" He waits a few beats. "What do you do with your conclusions, Officer Delaney?"

*Get people killed, nothing, save a girl's life, nothing, solve the case, nothing, raise a sleeping monster, nothing, shoot my only friend in the head-* "Nothing."

"Nothing?" That eyebrow goes up, and that's a good sign, isn't it? He isn't bothering to use the robot face on me.

I try a smile, but it feels too tight. "Do I look like badge and gun material to you? Some kind of supersize Jane Tracey with bad glasses? This isn't my mild mannered alter ego, sir, this is really me; bad knees, diabetes and all." He looks like he can't decide whether to apologize or not, and I have to laugh. Pity, I'm used to, but I'd rather have scorn; it chafes less.

"The point is, I'm smart enough to take an interest in these cases, but I'm also smart enough to keep my fat ass out of them in every official capacity." I finish off my coffee in a gulp, the sweetener less awful now it's gone cold. "I'm no wannabe gumshoe. The only reason I bother qualifying at the firing range is because it's departmental policy, and I don't need to give Hayden even more reasons to hassle me."

"I did notice you aren't wearing a sidearm."

I don't shudder, and though my right hand aches with memory, I manage not to clench it under the table. "I don't own one," I say, doing my best not to think of the narrow box taped to the bottom shelf of rack 40 down in the Hole. That's Chris's piece, not mine. I'm just hiding it, that's all. In case.

It's tempting to babble into the waiting silence that follows, and I figure that's exactly what it's there for, so I don't. After awhile, the AI guy sighs and checks his files again. "All right then; Detective Hayden learned of your interest in his case, he came down to the Evidence locker to confront you, and then what?"

I make myself shrug. "He did." Again, that waiting silence. This time, I crack first. "He tore my notebook in half, and told me to keep out of his business and let him do his job."

"In those words?" he asks, already knowing better.

"He said, 'Do I come down here when you're trying to work and knock the donut out of your mouth?'" He checks his file, and that not-smile peeks out, so I go on and admit it. Sexual harassment is the least of Hayden's worries, really. "Only he didn't say donut."

"No," he muses, not looking at me, "He didn't. And your reply?"

I don't see why this is necessary, but there's no point being shy at this stage of the game. "I told him if he got out of the closet and did something about his dick obsession, he'd have time to do his job properly." I toss the Styrofoam cup into the trash by way of a hint, in case he needs it. "That's when he broke his hand."

"Detective Hayden assaulted you?"

*Yes.*

"No. He punched the wall. It's cinderblock down there."

"Witnesses seem to disagree with you," he challenges, "I have three statements that he swung on *you,* not the wall."

I wish I hadn't pitched the cup. I wish I hadn't broken Hayden's hand. I wish I hadn't come to work. I wish I'd broken his skull instead. "Witnesses were at the other end of the hall, sir, and are therefore unreliable. Have you seen the lighting down in the Hole? Caves are brighter."

Again, the look. Again, the silence. He sets his pen down and laces his fingers again. I'm learning his signature moves. "Officer Delaney, does Detective Hayden frighten you?"

And if this question had been laid before me a year ago, I would have laughed. Because a year ago, I didn't *know* what frightened me. I hadn't seen it yet. Hadn't looked into its blue eyes and heard it explaining itself in clear, reasonable tones with blood all over its hands. Hadn't almost found myself believing it was right. Now, the question just makes my stomach cramp. I don't bother to hide the shudder as I answer once more with the truth.

"No, sir. No, he doesn't."

~*~

With Hayden in the penalty box, I expect the department to be buzzing once the AI guy's finally let me go, and buzzing it is. But instead of the Munchkin town glee club, the Blue Hive is alive and on point – a frenzied sense of everyone needing full hands, somewhere to go at top speed, some task that can stand up to the combination of adrenaline and irrelevance. A thick musk of ferocity, awe, and a half-guilty joy eddies through the whispering efficiency.

I don't need to see the dispatch report to guess what it means. After three years and fourteen bodies washed up on Fortress Point's ragged headland, my guts now divine the portents in icy knots and the ghost of a breakfast I didn't eat. Only one thing could have half the shift at full speed while the other half is conspicuously absent; the thing they've all been waiting for, because they didn't know it wasn't going to happen.

I close my eyes and try to remember the tidal charts from my notebook. Was the cave exposed early? Did something shift in the offshore deeps to draw the waters back, some sub-marine slouch or surge we'd never have felt on land? Something vast and unseen rising toward the air- *Shut UP!*

"Still got that notebook, Agent Harriet?" someone calls as they jostle past me. "Looks like the game's afoot again."

Cops. Who else can mix Fitzhugh with Doyle in the same line and keep a straight face? I work up a smirk and head toward the stairs. "Nah, Hayden's confiscated it so he could try and find his own ass."

A burst of laughter, and another voice chimes in. "He'll be using it awhile then."

"At least until he looks on his head," I reply, and their laughter follows me down the stairs. It means nothing. Hayden means nothing. This sudden, hollow popularity means nothing. There's another body, and though it's too early by a week for the currents to have carried it out, it must have turned up where the

106

others did, and in similar condition to justify all this. That *can't* mean nothing. It just can't.

For a crazy moment, I wonder if Hayden didn't kill this one, just to keep the case hot. Some diversion to brush aside Monday's stupidity. But no. He's neither that smart, nor that crazy. Not like Chris was.

I turn my cel phone on and the voicemail jangles at once. Steph's called five times in an hour. Someone must have had his radio on in the café when the dispatch call went out. Either that, or the newsies got wind of it, and I can expect to see the cute brunette from Channel 3 chewing over the gristle on the breakroom TV.

I don't call her back. I've got nothing to tell her, have I? I do ring the bakery down the block and order two dozen mixed though. The delivery boy will have to carry the boxes through the department on his way down to the Hole, and that'll bring the news to me faster than any subtle snooping could do. And I'll be the one to document the evidence, which with one little code I was never supposed to have, will give me ranking access to the case file as it develops.

I don't have a Detective playing fairy godmother now, it's true. But I also don't have a psycho grooming me for his sidekick; teaching me what to do, when, and worst of all, why. Theoretically this ought to be easier now. Safer, at least. Saner doesn't bear thinking.

I wonder if I can stonewall Steph long enough for the coroner's report to come online. No, she's used to getting her way. She won't let me hide too long, and so I've got to make best use of the time I have. Sort this out. Have my hypothesis in place before I have to face the froth of panic in her water-green eyes, and somehow convince her that things will be okay.

Patience. Observation. That's how I figured it out last time, and whatever's going on now, I'll sort it out just like last time, but better. Whatever's happened, whoever's done it, this time I'll know before I find myself facing my best friend over the sights of his gun, with no backup, nobody to stop his knife hand. Nobody but me. This time I won't need to go down to the water to know what's hatching out of it.

Maybe now would be a good time to get the gun out of its hiding place. I can stash it in my bag, keep it closer to hand, for awhile. A week, maybe. Two. Just in case.

~*~

"It's the same guy," the admitting clerk insists. "Two victims found nude at the same dumpsite on the same schedule. It's our guy."

Carew from Vice begs to differ. "It's not the same. Tourists' kids gone missing from a family boating trip, not skid row washouts." And he's right. Chris was never that careless.

His partner backs him up. "Sister and brother this time too. Even when we found more than one at a time, there's never been a male before."

*There was a male last year.* I don't say it. Because that wasn't a proper sacrifice, was it? It was just a deluded psycho Police Detective, shot down in a seaside grotto and left for the tide. That wouldn't have turned the key, wouldn't have jammed the door.

*Wouldn't it? Really?*

It's not him. It's just not. The currents take anything in the bay to the headland anyhow. And it's too early. None of the previous victims died before the Solstice, or were found before Christmas. It can't be him.

But Ellis from the trace lab thinks differently. "It's him. The eyes. No way that was fish or crabs, not with the bodies so very fresh. It has to be him."

108

Welkin is officer of the watch, and he's having none of it. "It's not him. The press knew about the eyes. People in China knew about the damned eyes. You show me those six cuts on the throats, and that weird shit with the hands, and I'll maybe buy it. But if it's just the eyes and lungs full of water? Pshh."

And he's right. Chris never drowned them. It's not the same. It's not him. Problem is, it's someone, and that someone could be trying to see Chris Dennis's work through. Someone could be trying to turn the key, only doing it wrong.

Amy comes over from the coroner's with several phials; hairs, nail scrapings, swabs. The ME's looking for sexual trace, and she's pretty sure he'll find it. That would nail the coffin shut on it being the Christmas Killer. If there was rape, then it's not anybody who'd bought into Chris's insane mythology.

I don't say that either. Nor do I enter into the debate over whether traces of sexual assault would even show up in a body that'd been in the sea for a week. I'm busy counting breaths to keep them absolutely level, and remembering to blink every other one.

The majority of the sidelined Blue thinks if there's any sexual component, then the perp will be someone trying to cover their own murders with the Christmas Killer's. An abuser tidying up before his toys can tell on him; an ex or a parent planning to cash in on celebrity victimhood by proxy; someone with a personal reason to want those two gone.

But could it not have been both? If they'd known what they would be locking out, why not make use of the silence?

*Doesn't this place make you dream, Michaela? These stones, this sea, this damned endless wind? Doesn't it give you patterns, night after night, that make such terrible sense? I see it in your eyes; you know why this is necessary. You know why this is right.*

109

I've been going in these circles all day. Every sliver of information sets me off again, every new rumor that follows the donuts down to the Hole, every note Hayden adds to the file, every murmur that slips through the ductwork between the Chief's office and the third floor bathroom.

I don't know what to think. By the end of my shift, I'm not even sure it couldn't have been Chris. Did I dream that shot? Was that shocked stare and tiny dark hole above it all in my imagination? Did I stop him, or just give him better cover? Did I shut a killer down, or did I set one free?

I want my notebook. I want to go over my notes on the tidal shifts, astrological conjunctions, and geological surveys of Sentinel Cove. I want to review my charmingly naive ponderings on the archaeological controversies surrounding its up thrust granite spars, like a henge above the thrashing sea. Paleolithic worship site? Stunning natural formation? Handy collusion of both? I want to read that line I wrote when it all fell into place, when the pattern of stars, tides, and crazy resolved into a sudden, bone-deep *knowing*. I want the comfort of proof that, even though led to it by a smiling killer, I still sorted this out once before.

But that hope is vain. Even if Hayden didn't burn it, Internal Affairs would snap the notebook up at the slightest hint of it still being around. It's part of an investigation, so it has to stay gone, for all the same reasons Chris has to stay gone – because it's far too complicated to still be around.

Still, there's something leaden heavy lodged in my belly when I close out my shift and head for the door. I pass Hayden's office, and overhear him phoning up the coast guard dive team to schedule a search in a new site. It should surprise me, perhaps, to realize I've the coordinates of Sentinel Cove memorized, but it doesn't.

It just makes me tired. It just makes me cold.

I am not surprised to see storm clouds gathering offshore when I finally make my way out to the bus stop.

~*~

*You ever hear of a skeleton key, Michaela?*
I shake the memory off like a dog shedding cold water, relieved when the thunderclap makes everyone on the bus jump too. The kid across the row keeps both hands and eyes on his phone, some stylish racket going on underneath the wires that link it to his ears. The man next to him glares as if the noise is my fault.

I stare back, unwinding the knotted straps of my bag from my bloodless fingers. I can't feel the metal through the canvas; there's this week's shift schedule and a dog-eared copy of *Something Wicked This Way Comes* between it and me. There's no whiff of gun oil, steel and malice when I shift the bag, and my murder weapon higher into my lap. He can't know I've got it. He's just glaring because he thinks I fell asleep on the bus, like a bum with the price of her fare and nowhere warmer to be at ten o clock a week before Christmas.

The way he holds my eye for a second before sniffing away tells me that. He doesn't know enough to be outraged. Or scared. Another time, I'd have laughed openly at him, or slipped in beside him and forced him into an excruciating ten minutes of small talk with the object of his scorn. That Mickey Delaney's long gone, it seems.

This Mickey Delaney has more pressing things to do with her transit time. Like deciding whether I'm really going to pull the cord in four stoplights', or let the Shoreline Café and the conversation with Steph roll on by. If I miss the stop, I can call from the apartment, apologize, claim weariness, be too damned drunk to discuss what we're going to do about two more dead kids when there were supposed to be none at all. Maybe if I stall, the decision of what to do will fall right out of my hands. That sounds much better than I know it should.

Funny; I never used to consider myself a coward.

Three more lights. The cord bumps my knuckles as the bus stops for the red. I should do it. Just get it over with, and quit hiding from ghosts and dreams. So why am I not taking hold of the cord?

A car pulls up next to the bus; low, square ended, the kind of thing they call 'classic' now, but they called 'gas guzzler' in the 80's, and 'POS land-yacht' in the 90's. Bowling alleys in front and back, pseudo leather over the top in a tired landscape of cracks and grit. And Steph in the passenger's seat.

Her hair's straggling out of its scrunchie, her uniform shirt's spotted with coffee and ketchup, and her pointed little chin's set hard as an ice breaker's prow. And she's riding shotgun in Detective Hayden's Oldsmobile.

"What are you doing?" I don't realize I've said it aloud until my breath fogs the glass. I scrub the haze away with my sleeve. "What the hell are you doing?"

She looks. Drawn by my movement, or the gravity of shock, she looks at the bus, gasps as she sees me. I don't want to see hope there again, not that twist-in-the-gut utter faith, and shaky-with-relief kind of fire that blazes up in those eyes. Whatever she's done, how can she think I'll know how to sort it out?

Her lips move, as though I could read her meaning across the gulf between us. Then she flinches, schools her face back to 'resolute', and turns to say something to the driver. I can see two taped-up fingers hovering over the steering wheel, the wrist brace a hollow gleam disappearing into his jacket. She nods, then claws the scrunchie out of her hair, shaking lazy curls free. In the haunted blue light of the dash I half expect them to float weightless around her head, but they settle on her shoulders, and then she smiles. Almost.

*Stephanie Nayatt, what the hell are you up to?*

The light changes, and despite my willing it, the bus can't keep up with the Olds' V8. They're out of sight by the time we're at the Café, and I dial into my voicemail in the hope that my prickling thumbs and pounding heart are somehow wrong.

The first five messages are just what I expected. Questions, panicky anger, desperation that must have flown like a red flag above her head. She learnt things as well over the day, from the same bored cops who'd stopped to gossip on their way home. The out-of-towner kids, the eyes, the clothes. And she made no better use of them than I had, though as her messages progressed, the fear bled out of her voice, and a savage, crafty note came in. I could almost hear the plan take root as she talked into the empty space where I had not been.

The last message was the important one.

*Mickey, we have to go back. Tonight, when the tide will be low enough to show the gate. It's the only way we'll know what this means, you know it is. We have to go back where it really happened to be sure no one's been there, or... we have to go see, or we'll drive ourselves nuts.*

A pause. A murmur from behind a muffling hand. A reply. Neither make any sense, then the line goes sharply clear again, and her voice is cold and cloudy as sea ice.

*"I'm going home after this shift. If I haven't heard from you by then, I'll... I'll find some other way to get out to Sentinel. But I need you to come, Mickey. You can't make me face that place alone, I know you can't. The paper said the eclipse starts at midnight, so come before then. We can get in and out before the light's gone, and...*

A sound, equal kin to a gasp, hiccup and death rattle. Then, *"You have to come, Mickey. Please."*

113

And then there's nothing more. The dead air is like a seashell to the ear, and I weather the urge to hurl the phone. The bus turns, and engine groaning at the strain, labors up Fenswych hill. I watch the Fortress Point harbor light as we climb, its beam winking as it sweeps the darkness.

On the other side of the bay, the moon perches bald faced and patient on the granite spars of Sentinel Cove. But as relentless as that cold glare seems now, the truth is even worse; there is only so long she will wait.

*Have you ever heard of a skeleton key, Michaela?*

Of course I have. One key is much the same as another, and any of them can open that sort of lock with a little time and patience. Unless someone else has put their own key into the lock from the other side, in which case the door stays closed fast for another year.

Or so the madman tried to tell me.

I make it out to the cove in just about two hours. Steph is waiting for me, perched on the Olds' trunk while the wind braids her hair with ragged streams of cigarette smoke. The ground at her feet is littered with spent butts. Far as I can tell, she's alone.

"Thought you weren't coming." Her voice is low, rough and thick, as though she's been crying. Or screaming.

I wave a hand at the moon mid-sky. "Nobody saw me," I tell her by way of explanation. The car's icy under my hip, but I'm exhausted, and my knee feels like it's fraying under my skin. The smoke slashes across my nose, and beneath the tobacco sear I can smell burning oil, oakum, and driftwood.

"Where's Hayden?"

She stares at me, the planes of her face gone sharp and alien in the moonlight, and for a moment I think she isn't going to answer. Then she's sliding across the trunk, cuddling close and draping herself like weed across my shoulder. "He went down already. Said he was going to check it out and make sure it was safe. You know how he is."

And I don't ask how he made the climb down those treacherous rock steps – not so smooth or level as in my dreams, not for centuries now, -- with his fingers taped and his wrist in a brace. I don't ask why her hair is damp as it whips across my neck, or why she smells of the salt spray that's pounding the rocks eighty-five feet below. I don't ask why I can't remember how I got her out of the cave and up the cliff with my crap knee. I don't ask why she never went home again.

And I don't ask her *"What have you done?"*

Because I don't want to, don't need to. I can feel, for a second, a jutting bulk of steel between breast and hip as she pillows against me. Then she's slipping off the car, one of my hands caught in hers as she tows me across the tarmac to the ruined overlook point.

"Creepy," she says, climbing onto the burnt out platform so she can look out over the water. The wind lifts her hair in wild flows behind her, and I cannot see her eyes to tell whether it's a joke or not. But then I'm not exactly laughing because it's funny.

"I meant the wind." She gives me her best disarming smile. In this strange stormlight, it looks like a rictus. "Almost sounds like something's screaming."

I join her on the unburnt half of the deck, but don't bother pretending to watch the storm. "Singing," I tell her, and she laughs.

"Singing, huh? What sings like that? Cats in a blender?"

Should I tell her she isn't actually fooling me?

"Mermaids." She giggles, but I press on. "Sirens, coming to air only when the moon's light can't blind them.  Swum up by thousands from the deeps to sing hymns to the God of all Storms."

It takes a moment for her to manage that laugh again. "Okay.  Mermaid carols.  Why not?  I like that better than wind over the chimney holes anyhow."  Then she ducks under the charred crossbeam, slithers around a concrete piling and draws up on the worn rock that heads the descent.  "We should get going before it starts to rain."

And yeah, I do have to follow.

The climb's easier, but maybe that's because my brain's had a year of dream-practice to learn the way.  The wind's just as fierce, but now I can spare the attention to listen properly, I can almost pick the melody line out of the chaos of wind and water.

The tide's fully out when I set my feet on the red stone path.  I can hear it fretting some dozen or two yards beyond the guardian stone.  The moonlight's is fading, her white face bruising up in creeping red shadow.  Not quite enough light to check the gun that's tucked into my own waistband, so I'll have to do it by feel.  Of Detective Hayden there is no sign.

Stephanie turns on the path.  "Mickey, what's wrong now? We don't have a lot of time here."

I search for her face in the bleeding light.  "Have you ever heard of a skeleton key, Steph?"

It feels like a test, and when she laughs at me and claps my shoulder to haul me along, I can't tell which of us passed it, and which of us failed.  And then she lets me go, fumbling out a flashlight as the moon's last sliver is conquered, and the storm reaches out to devour the remains.

"You know I love you, Mickey Delaney," she says as the fierce, false light chases all trace of human warmth from her face, "But you've got too many ghosts.  Sometimes I swear it seems like you never left this place at all."  Then she turns away and slashes her way through the cave mouth's darkness, leaving me to follow with a dead man's gun burning cold in my hand.

I cycle a bullet into the chamber, and count my potential shots from memory, saving out the very last bullet for me.

"I didn't leave," I say to the wind, the sea, and the dark-faced moon. "Not really."

# Mrs. Harker Instructs Her Daughters as to the Ways of Men and Vampires.

## A Satire in Five Sonnets.

### 1

Take care, oh beware, oh my curious daughters;
Go cautious and quiet and shy
When perils pursue thee from shadowy quarters
You're lost in the flash of an eye.

Oh, a husband is one thing; a fortune and name
And these you must seek, it is true,
But a fortune is chaste and serene in its claim
And the stakes are much higher for you.

For we have a kernel hid deeply within,
Of sulphurous corruption and shame;
Let but one careless stroke spark its tinder to singe,
And your worth will expire in the flame!

Just think of your bonnets and dresses of lace
Besmirched with the ash and decay
Which is all t'will remain of the virtue and grace,
And repute you'll have frittered away.

For some sins cannot be amended
No matter how deeply repented.

That hunger, once kindled, fills up all your sight
And it greedily clamors for more
The wanting will give you no moment's respite;
You'll crave only things best deplored.

You'll be as a she-wolf, a succubus-beast
Indulging unspeakable lusts
Who will steal little children, on innocence feast
And who burrows her nest in the dust.

Oh no, titter not, my sweet daughters of quality
Trust me, this is danger most real;
The world's full of those who devour maidens' frailty
And crave all this ruin to deal,

And would waken within you a beast of their stripe,
Which cares nothing for civilized rule
But which takes what it chooses wherever it likes
And names folk of quality 'fools'.

What manner of life would that be?
For no one invites monsters to tea.

## 3

Good girls thus despoiled creep as wolves in the gloaming,
Strong men into bedlamites turn,
One moment incautious, one unwary roaming,
Whereafter the fallen are spurned

By the world, by the daylight, by all that is holy
By family, home, and the grave.
They plummet, their infamy daily unfolding;
Once virtuous, henceforth depraved.

And my dears, once the spark has caught fire within you
No force can restrain it again.
Though you garland your windows, set mirrors to guard you
Or hide behind crucified men;

You can never be trusted, not e'en by the man
Who would have you in spite of the stain;
For let only the vampire reach out his foul hand
And you will take up the refrain.

As Eve in the garden did err.
Think not yourself stronger than her.

## 4

No, best, in the end, that you stay ever maids
And you ne'er become women at all;
That the fire remain quenched under ruffles and braids,
Merry tea parties, visits, and balls.

And when you are wedded, think only of England,
Your duty, and maybe the pain
With blood and disgust keep your evil unquickened,
And firmly forever restrained.

But if one should seek thee with dark eyes alight,
And with appetites foreign and strange,
Or appear in your dreams as a mist in the night,
You'll have only yourself for the blame

When you find that the ones who did love you betimes
Must now hunt you to ground like a beast;
Abjure you with fire and fists for your crimes
And drive thick shanks of wood through your breast.

They will weep to have treated you so,
But daughters, their duty they know.

For they merely defend, as it's just that men ought,
The full rights which the Lord has made theirs
Like the hunting, the killing, the logic of thought
And, of course, the begetting of heirs.

And any usurper engenders their rage
And inspires them as hounds to the chase,
To extinguish your fire and their honor assuage,
Leaving shame branded plain on your face.

So now, my sweet daughters, for all of your days
Seek nothing but that which you ought;
True, freedom and passion and power may blaze
But you'll find they are too dearly bought.

Nay, cleave to your dolls, and your innocent pleasures,
Play only as good children should.
Then you'll be protected, beloved and treasured
And perfectly well understood.

Take the learning, my daughters, from me;
Never trust that which makes thee too free.

# Dead Language

It was not like Cellini, he told himself, rubbing his handover the pitted stone, pressing his tacky fingers along inscriptions that skittered away from the eye, and hid in shadow, lichen, and sedimentary swirls; this was not a case of ego lashed over avarice by way of plausibility.

He had known when he took the codex from the appalling little shop, that he did not "deserve" it, per se, and if the pawnbroker had not wished to sell it to him, he did not deceive himself that it was anything but her right to refuse. The Codex Oceanus was hers, however she had come by it, and he did not trouble himself with outrage at her implication that she would sooner sell a toddler a land mine; she was hardly ignorant of the stele's importance, its significance, and while her superstitions were inconvenient to him, they hardly justified his own … crime.

He had not been pushed to it, but had simply discovered in that breathless moment, what he was capable of when suitably inspired. He had discovered his price. And, well, didn't every man have one, after all? It could be taken for a point of pride that his was for knowledge, not for gold.

There… just where the clockwise line branched off to curl over the corner; was that the reed-pressed tick marks of cuneiform he felt? He turned that side to the light, squinted, peered, and could not be sure.

The stone was porous, pitted as though from acid rain or the scouring desert winds. The texture presented both a baffling complication to making out the inscriptions, and to cleaning the stele's thick heel. Water had not lifted the stain, merely swirled a little pink clockwise down the drain, and made the small apartment reek of metal and marshes. The stone took on the water, though, with a sudden sanguine bloom, as though drinking the stain in through its pores. The rusty sediment stood out handsomely now, branching in a kind of weightless arc like smoke in still air, or ink in a full glass. The inscriptions, he realized now, followed the lines of pigment within the stone – a brilliant artifice, worthy of Michelangelo. The angel within the stone lay there still, trapped and dumb, but its ruddy skin prickled with nearly-lost secrets when held in reverent hands just so.

He shook himself free of the fancy with a shudder. The stele seemed heavier now, though it had been plenty heavy before. Not granite, then. Some kind of coral? He set it on the desk blotter and went to collect his papers, the book, a magnifying glass, and a stronger light – he was going to need them all.

The pawnbroker was sitting in his chair when he returned, ruffled and furious, and thoroughly alive. A part of him was relieved. Another part of him was somewhat surprised at this relief, and wondered just why he was not more surprised. Still another part of him cared nothing for any of this, and was merely glad he had brought his revolver along with him from the office. "You're not taking it back," he told her, pointing.

"Damn straight I'm not," she answered. He blinked, and her lips twisted into a smile that cracked the dried blood on her cheek. "Trust me, Professor, I have no intention of touching that thing ever again at this point. You forget – I bought the thing from the last descendant in the first place."

"The last descendant," he scoffed. She was nothing like old enough to have done so. The cities had not even been rediscovered until seismic activity had thrust the ruins up out of the ocean off Japan. Not even the earliest Chinese histories ranged far enough back to hint at what had been found there when the oceans gave way.

"Her name was Kaimei. She'd learned the tongue by ear, as had every one of her kindred before her," the woman went on, sitting calm and prim in his chair. "In her last days she summoned me to her bedside so it would not die along with her. I know what that is, how it works, better than you can guess, even with your...

124

book." The desk light casting her tawny skin and delicate features into savage relief as she flicked one finger at the brittle leather volume under his arm. Her hair, gleaming black and smooth rumpled up strangely on one side, as though the blood had dried while she lay on it. "And that's what I came to tell you, Professor," she said, rising from the chair and turning to go, "You've done it entirely wrong."

"Stop," he stammered as she turned her back on him, "You stop there!" But when she obeyed, he couldn't think what to ask. "How did…What do you…" he shook his head to banish all the foolish questions with obvious answers. Then he stepped toward her, thumb pulling back the pistol's hammer. "Tell me what you mean by that; that I've done it wrong."

She didn't fully turn, but the hue of her light-caught glance was so arresting that he nearly missed her reply. "The Codex won't work for you with _my_ blood on it. The Teachers expect a student to pay his own way."

His heart lurched in his chest. Foolish, yes. Wholly, and entirely unsympathetic to his decades of education in the cool patterns of science. He glanced at the stele, noted how the red patterns in the stone _were_ more pronounced near the stained base, and only noticed the pawnbroker's retreat once she was close enough to open the door. "Wait! What do you mean by-"

"I've told you already," she cut him off with another sidelong, predator's glance, "It's an _oral_ tradition. To learn it, you must summon those who can speak it." She stepped through the door, as though she didn't care about his gun at her back.

"And then?"

"And then they speak," the pawnbroker said, "And you listen for as long as you can."

Then she pulled shut the door behind her.

125

# Necromancy

"Fucking hell Ramona," Trini says from the bedroom door.

It's usually the first thing out of her mouth when she sees her mother these days. Five years ago, when she'd first come back to the house and its madness, the phrase had often sounded appalled, disgusted, outraged, terrified, and sometimes grudgingly amused. Now weariness is all she can muster, aside from a little nausea and concern for her shoes.

"Hell, we just replaced the carpet last month," she grumbles, slipping off the sandals and tossing them back to relative safety in the hallway. Her feet, she can wash; Jimmy Choos are another thing altogether. "Why you always got to have cream carpet when you know you're just gonna do this crap?" she asks, picking her way around the bed's remains, now a fluffy tangle of sheets, feathers, mattress ticking, and foam. The mirror that had once hung over the headboard dusts the whole thing in silver -- there's a bullet hole the diameter of her thumb in its empty frame. No sign of the gun, but she doesn't much feel like searching for it.

Ramona isn't in the bed, but Pony and Elvis are, out cold and wearing matching gladiator costumes. Nestled between them is that new fashion model, the Italian one who doesn't look older than fifteen. She's got precisely spaced razor cuts up her belly and breasts, a faint line of white dust along her inner thigh, and the smile of a beatified saint on her bony face. Far as Trini can tell, all three are still breathing, so she leaves them there and goes to turn off the taps that are flooding the bathroom.

Ramona is there, either, though half her wardrobe is, a soggy cascade of sequins, feathers, and designer nonsense, each costing more than her own car. Ruined now, but not hiding her mother's drowned corpse beneath their glittering disarray. Trini isn't sure whether she's relieved or disappointed. When she opens the patio door, and spots the unmistakable thatch of bottle-blonde hair over the top of one of the pool lounges, it ticks a little closer to the disappointed side. Trini firmly squashes it and goes to check that her mother is still among the living.

And of course, she is -- Ramona Bones, mortal coil unshuffled; a resplendent ruin of a woman, Teflon-livered, rehab proof, as brittle as her name. She sprawls, in drooling collapse and a dress apparently made of bacon, beside the pool... into which someone driven a Smart Car.

"Where's the paparazzi when you need them?" Trini grumbles to herself, checking that the neighboring lounger is more or less clean before sitting. Times like this, she almost wishes she smoked, just so she'd have something to do while procrastinating. Aside, that is, from wishing she'd never let herself be talked into leaving school, leaving Boston, leaving sanity to come home to... this. To more a zoo than a home; to a shallow pond of sycophants and parasites whose job it was to make their host feel young while draining her dry; to a famous, fabulous idiot of a woman lying in a puddle of her own sick while her dress melts obscenely in the rising sun.

"Not enough therapy in the world..." Trini sighs, and turns her mother's face to the light.

Judging by the greyish cast under the warpaint, she guesses Ramona's good for at least one more volley of spew. The lounger was probably the best place for her, barring rehab. And what luck that her mother chose a propped loungers to pass out into, rather than flat on her back. She might have drowned otherwise -- accidentally brought the whole grotesque feeding frenzy to an ignominious close as she joined the illustrious company of Jimi, Dorsey and Bonham in the posh *pulmonary aspiration* club in the sky.

Ignominious. Trini huffs a joyless laugh -- a $20 word for a two bit freakshow, Ramona would have said.

*Twenty twenty twenty four hours to go-o-o, I wanna be sedated!* Trini jumps as the tinny ghost of Joey Ramone splits the

127

morning quiet. *Nothing to do, nowhere to go-ooo.* The cell phone vibrates under the lounger, mercifully beside, rather than actually in the puddle of sick. Its screen shows a smiling fat man. Trini thumbs it open before Joey gets to the line about the wheelchair.

"Murray," she says. Greeting enough, all things considered.

"How you feeling, dollface?" comes the reply, "Getting yourself moneyed up for the interview? We're gonna give the old hometown crowd a good ass kicking, I tell you. Show 'em you still know how to rock-"

"Murray, it's Trinidad."

"Kiddo?" His voice goes over all chummy and plummy; half politician, half drug store Santa. "Good God, you sound just like your old lady! You gonna steal her show one day, mark my words, Kiddo. You remember your uncle Murray when you're famous, eh."

She manages not to scoff, though it's a near thing. "Look, Mom had a party here last night..."

Murray swears quietly in German.

"Yeah. Pretty much. Everything's a wreck, including Mom. There's a dog in the bathtub. I don't know whose. I don't know if-"

"How bad?"

She cuts a look at Ramona, noting the grayish tint to her lips. "Well, let's just say if that interview's earlier than ten tonight, it's probably best she doesn't show up for it."

"Princess, the *show's* at nine!"

"Yeah." It's all she can say. She lays her head back against the lounger and closes her eyes to the rising sun's blaze – honey and gold over the pool. Later, it will be a white hammer pounding LA down to dust, but right now it almost feels like hope.

128

"Look," Murray sounds like he's sweating already. "Look, princess, we can fix this. I need you to go into your ma's room, and get out the jewelry box with the-"

With the emergency stash of cocaine in the lining; five slim little syringes with very long needles beneath a bit of velvet and cardboard. Trini's stomach turns over, but she keeps her voice bored. "It's gone, Murray." And then again, into the horrified silence, "It's gone. She found it months ago."

"And you didn't tell me?"

"No point. You'd bring more, you'd hide it, she'd just find it again." Ramona stirs, makes a fretful noise, and suddenly Trini is on her feet and shouting. "She always finds it, Murray! Always! She finds it, and she takes it, and when she's out, she takes something else! You can't just medicate this away whenever you need her to make you some more money!"

She kicks the lounger, knowing her bare foot will bear the mark of it, but past caring, really. Past caring if she bruises, past caring if she bleeds, past caring if she breaks her own bones so she can never walk away again. Past caring when the support bar breaks and the lounger slaps Ramona Bones flat down with a lurch and a groan; lookouts clapped on paradise, as the song says, soul bound just contrariwise.

"She's killing herself," Trini says, turning from the grisly sight. "And you're both making me watch. I want to go home."

She knows what he will say. She's the best assistant Ramona Bones ever had. The only one she can trust. Her mother needs her. He needs her. The press. The fans. Nobody wins if something like this gets into the papers. They'll sort it all out once they get her on her feet. After she's managed this one more show. This one more interview. This one more comeback album, then they'll intervene, he promises. They'll get Ramona help, and make her get better it, he promises.

He always promises. It's his job, promising, and he's good at it.

Trini thumbs the phone shut, and then for good measure tosses it into the pool. Murray's office is across the valley, the radio station even farther out. Even if he'd called her from the road, rush hour traffic will have him stalled for a good 45 minutes – assuming he doesn't have to detour in order to pick up some magic Make Ramona Bones Act Like She's Alive medicine.

"You're not alive," she says to the Ruin by the pool. "You've been a singing corpse for… Christ, I don't even know how long. Or if you ever were alive."

Ramona makes a low sound, guttural and thick. A zombie moan perfectly in keeping with her melting decay.

It'll take her twenty minutes to pack, Trinidad knows. She's packed to leave so many times in the past five years, she's practically worn grooves in the lining of her luggage. The escape money is taped inside her guitar, just in case she can't get to her bank account. Because with Ramona, you never know.

Now, Trinidad knows. The calm sun tells her with certainty that this day – this one right now, is the one when everything changes. Judgment day. The end of the world.

"Maybe you had a pulse once," she says as she turns from the gurgling creature that had stopped being her mother when neither of them was paying attention, "but now you're nothing but an appetite and an ego. I'm done watching you rot. Dig your own way out of the grave from now on."

On the way out of the house, she thumbs the security system's panic button, leaving a clear, un-smudged print. The phone in the house begins to ring, desperate for reassurance, and Trinidad Bones smiles to herself. No password this time. Everything is not okay.

But it's going to be.

# Nine to Five

She showed the back of her fist, and uncurled one finger. "The woman who cleaned our house. My father paid her, before he went," her lip twisted, irony and disgust in equal measure. "to hide me from the authorities. When the police came to search her house, they did not even give her the chance to speak. They just shot her in the hallway and stepped over."

The pretty blonde agent frowned, nervous. "About your father, Mrs.-"

"In the throat. One bullet. I was in the coat closet, looking through the keyhole. The blood ran under the door before I could get off my knees. They found me covered in it."

She uncurled two more fingers, bleach rough, nail bitten, white and trembling. "The two officers who were bringing me for questioning. The Americans rammed their car to get to me. One died right then. The other had time to get out his gun, but they killed him, two shots to his head through the window. Do you know, I still dream about tasting his blood?"

The agent went white, and she nodded. "Yes. I was screaming. I tell myself I spat out only broken glass, not shards of bone, but some nights I am not convinced."

The second agent came back in. Martini, she remembered, like the drink. Dark, bearded, wearing toughness like a coat he would take off when it no longer suited him. His every move as he folded his arms and leaned against the doorframe made it clear; she was meant to fear him. And so she ignored him and kept her eyes on the blonde as she uncurled a fourth finger.

"There was a tour bus. The agents got us onto it with the other tourists, and we rode it to the border town. The driver didn't know he was committing treason -- he had no idea who I was, or that the man and woman with me were not my parents. He would have recognized my father's name, if anyone had said it to him, but he had no way to know that I was a prize he demanded in his terms -- the guarantee of his 'loyalty' to his new country."

"You were in danger," Agent Martini said, gesturing with the file he had gone out for. It was a fifth the size of the one they'd had when the interview began. "As the only child of a defecting Nobel prize winner, your life would have been-"

She waved him silent without a look. "That bus driver's family never saw him again after that day. I wrote to them after we were settled here, asked after him many times, until they stopped writing back. He just did his job. He just drove the bus, and he betrayed his country doing it."

She uncurled her thumb, and then brought up the other fist, and added three fingers to the count from there. Neither agent interrupted this time. "The farmer, his wife, their two sons. I never learnt their names. They did not even know we were in their barn that day. They could not have given us up to the soldiers even if they had wanted to, but they were all killed anyway. I saw the whole farm burning from the middle of the lake -- house, barn, shed, everything. The farmer had a boat, you understand. The agents wanted it for a night crossing, so we would pass no armed checkpoints at the border."

She drew a deep breath, and fancied she could smell smoke in the sterile little meeting room. The agents traded a look which as much as said, 'get her back on track,' and she glowered at them both in turn. Then she raised one more finger.

"I was in school then. I was going to sing opera. I was going to be a star, and be famous for creating beauty on the stage, rather than for creating death on the battlefield like my father. I was going to light up the world, but in two weeks, I went from Prima Donna to Plague Ship. Everyone who had known me, who had been close, or even kind to me all fell under suspicion. Their lives were scarred, their careers were ruined. My Singing Master was a *genius!"*

She brought her open hand down, slam on the table, so Bellamy jumped and ruffled the neatly squared file before her. "He was a genius, and I was his finest pupil, and because of my Father's greed for power, and your country's greed for military glory, and a political coup against my homeland, that brilliant man died in a prison camp. He never taught anybody to sing again." She looked down at her hand, and lowered its rough, chapped mate to lie beside it. "And instead of lighting up the stage with the gifts he taught me, I am cleaning toilets for minimum wage so your National Security Agency won't have to worry about me attracting too much ... attention."

She flicked a corner of the file as though it were a bloated carrion fly. "And apparently, my father is still strangling prostitutes when he is not in his laboratory."

"You knew what he was all along." It was not a question. Agent Bellamy did not bother to hide the horror in her voice or her face, and for that, she respected her a little.

She nodded. "It was why I got away from him as fast as I could. First at home, and then here."

"Because a pathology like his doesn't begin with killing, or with abusing strangers," Martini said, clinical and cold, as though discussing the weather or his lunch. "He is all about control in every phase of the murder, and he would have been like that for all your life, getting more and more abusive as his desires grew."

Her stomach twisted, and she let it show on her face. "I told the agents they were bringing home a monster, that they would regret it if they let him stay." She pinned the blonde's gaze with her own. "Do you know what they said?" A headshake, tight and tiny as a flinch. She returned it with a smile she knew could only be cruel. "They said they would put a note in their report."

The other agent unfolded his arms, tucked the folder down by his side, and she tracked the movement with her eyes. "Did you find such a note in my file, agent Martini? Or was that blacked out by your NSA censors before you got it?"

Martini scowled, but this time it was Bellamy who cut in with accusation in her voice. "Michelle Juan went missing within a year of your father's gaining American citizenship. You were still living with him on the airbase then."

She frowned, then understood. "Yes, I suspected. Yes, he knew I suspected. He dared me to try and tell. He called the State Department. Put the phone in my hand and told me I could say whatever I wanted to them, and just see what they would do about it." She felt herself shaking, the memory of helpless rage as hard to swallow now as it had been then.

"What did you say to them?"

She glowered at Martini, not fooled by his gentle tone. "I said it was a wrong number. Then I got out of his house as soon as I could find a job. I married the first American who said he would have me, and moved as far away as your government would let me go. I haven't seen my father, or spoken to him in five years. I can't help you find him now."

"Please," agent Bellamy caught at her hand, skin cloying and smooth before she yanked away. "Please try and help us. He's killed five innocent young women, and their families deserve-"

"Nine."

A blink, doe-eyed and gleaming, shocked as though the agent had been slapped.

"The cleaning woman; the two police officers; the bus driver; the farmer; his wife; two sons; my Master. Nine innocent people died because of me. Because of *him*. Nine good people whose families had to bury them as traitors, and act ashamed of them for the rest of their lives. Nine people died to bring me to America, agent Bellamy, and all because my father said he would

134

not stay and work here if they did not fetch me to him. All that blood on me! On *my head.*" She drew a shaking breath, and had to close her eyes to manage the words. "Nobody even once asked me if I wanted to come here."

"I'm. I'm so sorry..."

She shoved the file, watched with grim satisfaction as the glossy, grisly photographs slithered out all over Agent Bellamy and the floor. "You Americans worked hard to win your monster. You have bought and paid for him in blood, and now you want to know where he is?" She shoved to her feet, not caring as the chair toppled behind her with a crash. "I have no idea, nor do I care. He's your monster now; find him yourselves."

She yanked open the office door, brushing past the man as though he was not half blocking the way. "And when you do find him," she called back as she strode past the rest of the agents, silent around their tables, maps and computer screens, "I suggest you put him down like the animal he is!"

"I'll make a note of it," Agent Martini called after her as she slammed out the door.

# The Moon in her House or, Why Cats Do Not Weep.

There have always been Tigers in the world, my love, even from the very first of days. Wherever Men have walked, there was one or another of that grand sort; Lions, Leopards, Lynx and golden Ounces; fleet Cheetah, Jaguar and Tigers without pity; all stalking proud-pawed and lordly through jungle, desert, peak, and plain. Men learnt well to fear them, for to such twilit lantern eyes a man is not much different from a deer, goat, or pig – save that he is often slower.

And how could men not wonder, eyeing the brindled flank of she who dozes in the sunlit window; the bundled haunch of he who hunts dust-mice beneath the sofa; the comfortable burr from she who warms a lap of a chill spring evening -- does it not make them wonder how such fierce allies as these could have come down from the trees and into their ancestor's feeble campfire light without making a feast of them all?

The answer's less to do with environmental adaptation, symbiotic domestication, and agrarian grain storage practices than dusty science likes to think. Bunk's sprung up like weeds to choke the gulf between Tiger and Tabby, Leopard and Longhair, Monster and Moggy, but bunk it remains.

The truth, my dear, is a secret – no, actually, it's a Secret. And in the tradition of Secrets, it must be whispered into the safest of ears, lest it chew and worry, and gnaw, and eat away at its bearer from the inside out, until only Death remains to know the truth of it. This is the manner of Secret that *must* be told, lest it kill by lingering poison, or lie forgotten until history coughs it up again, ripe, fermented, and dangerously heady. Whole worlds can become drunk on such Secrets, Beloved; drunk enough to burn.

Of course your wits are sound, your tongue well minded, and your shoulders look fit to bear up the truth of it. So come and sit close, warm and Fire-warded with me; pillow your head upon breathing fur, and I will tell you how the Queen of Secrets came to our lonely little world.

It was long, and long ago when she burst out, sleek and brilliant on the last gasp of light from a far and desperate star. He flung her forth, this dying star, hurled her far from the darkness which closed him around, and hoped, perhaps, his legacy might see her to some better end than his. We may judge of that star now only by the fine, silver claw which remains; this little Queen, this quicksilver glimmer; furred thicker than comet's hair, but warm as a sunrise glow. She was nimble and silent on velvet feet, with a ken for which way's up, and a knack for keeping those feet pointed the other. Well versed, also, in the making of one thing from the breaking of another, sprung, as she had, from the confluence of Death and all Secrets the old Star had known.

She was born knowing her own name, and tell me, beloved, what other creature draws first breath so wise as that? But her father-star did not stir when the little Queen spoke it, though the Name raised bristling barbs upon her tongue, and whetted her teeth sharp and long.

Comets roved through the old sun's grave, bristling and portentous, but they had no ear for the small Queen, being temperamental, easily insulted, and never fully trustworthy. They ruffled her tail frizzy and fat, but she let them pass by. The rocky bones that paved the old sun's grave only rattled, lifeless when she bespoke them. Amusing toys the dead, cold things might be, but the game did not satisfy the burning urge to speak, to sing, to know, and to tell the Truth of things aloud.

Thus, the Queen resolved to wander.

And wandering, found her way to where a new, young Sun was King and very Yellow. He gathered shining great jewel-worlds in dancing patterns around him, and being a young and serious Sun, he concerned himself chiefly with their patterns, not with the silvery Queen who poked and patted and nosed out the Secrets from each.

Oh, delight, to shave ice with her tongue, and taste volcanoes hidden deep within; to brush her starfire whiskers through softly humming clouds, and fret eye storms like mice across their brindled surface; to sweep tail through dust-banded fields, and clatter asteroids like seedpods in her wake; to rake her claws through chill dust in all the colours of things that bleed!

But there was one jewel – one of the Yellow King's treasures which held treasures of its very own. And can we wonder, Sweetling, that the little Queen should find her way here, where great trees flocked slow and stately across velvet plains? Where mountains joust the blooming clouds across the face of forever, and oceans pearl the green with empyrean blue? Can we wonder that her wise little nose should lead her to where the first men huddled small and brown at the flanks of their campfires and watched the darkness as though it held not wonders, but only Death? And finding such a mystery there in the skirts of the night, how can we wonder that our fierce Queen should decide to stay?

In those days, you know, Mankind's ken was different to what it is today. They knew the daytime was their strength – that they were beloved of the Golden King, and while not precisely protected by his brilliant regard, at least measurably safer while he held his course in the sky. And they understood that Fire loved them also, as much as she was able, and would consent in his absence to give them light, heat, and what protection she could.

And Death – oh, Death did those men know far better than they wished. Death had swift paws, quick, sharp hooves, and antlers eager to show blood to the air. Death tasted bitter as spring berries, or too-bright toadstools. Death roared like water in narrow canyons, like tumbling snow on steep slopes, like stormlight hammering the ground in violet rage, like howling night hunters no Firelight can reveal. Death stung like papery scorpions, unseen underfoot, like weavers with more legs than patience, like honey-hoarders, serpents, and stone-headed spears. Death screamed like great eagles in stoop, an Ounce aloft ranging her leap, like a heavy branch tearing loose far overhead. Death was the color of nighttime, all men knew this; it was vast, pitiless, patient, and hungry, and it ruled all things that the Sun left to darkness.

All things, of course, but Fire.

Death was bigger in those days than it is now. It came to the Firelight wardings of Men, as a single, solid darkness. It bat-wing whispered that fuel might burn faster than planned, and run out before dawn. It panther-growled that rain might come, and douse the flames. It snatched with thorny legs those not close enough to the light, and dragged them away so quick there was no scream, only a gulp of surprise and then Death's sated sigh. Oh, tyrant is the Steward when the King cannot attend! Oh, cruel is he that cannot rule but for another's say! Oh, merciless the whispering dark when naught was left to burn!

What could men do, in such straits, but try to appease the great unseen? Death cared not for gold or jewels though; it wanted no sacrament of soft pelts, bright beads or steel, but Secrets -- oh, Secrets were sweet! Trickling from nerve-parched tongues at the Firelight's wavering edge, sipped from cold lips and swallowed down, never to gurgle into Knowing again.

(The first Secret Death ate was of what exactly Death wanted with Secrets, the birthright of all who walked the Earth, to begin with. Perhaps Death was building a great, rustling hoard of them, or twisting and braiding them into armor, all glittering spikes and searing hooks – for what is more painful than Truth, except a Secret abused? Perhaps it merely took them in, crunched them up small, savored their Knowing that none save itself should Know again. Death is greedy, after all – that Secret is very well known, even to this day.)

So let us imagine what our Silver Queen saw when she followed her whiskers down to the satin sands. Let us picture night, thick and black as was nothing else in the world – it will do to picture the belly of the deepest cavern, where even now, some wise part of you knows, Death lurks still. That is almost darkness enough. Imagine sand, warm with sunlight's memory under tender paws, but air so chilly dry, it tears breath from between the teeth, and spins it into steam unseen. Imagine whispers of grass and possibly voices; rattle of scrub or of chattering teeth that tickle your ears on the breezeless air. Imagine the smell of still water and sand, and of green things growing, but no glimmer of sight, no shimmer of light to show you where these things might be. Death was big enough in those days to block out even the watchful stars.

Still, our little Queen was kitted for blackness and cold, having traveled quite some time in the void. She merely fluffed up her silvery fur, tucked her paws to the warm sand, and waited.

And soon enough, Death crept up, close and curious to the silvery gleam. "You are not very big," it said, all growl and gloat.

"I am big enough," the Queen answered, and flicked a spark from one ear.

"I have eaten things twenty times the size of you," Death said, a rattle of bone and failing breath. "Mighty hunters with teeth like sabers; Mammoth mountains of muscle and bone; Camels, sloth and bison have I taken by thousands, and here you sit alone. What's to stop me eating you as well?"

At that, the Queen opened one eye, green as her old Sun's last gasp, and flexed her claws in the sand. "Do try," she invited, politely showing her neat, pointed teeth.

"You are too far for the Fire to save you," Death said, intrigued at that viridian glance, but beginning to guess that here sat more than just a queer, small creature. "There stands a high dune between, and you are quite alone. But I will spare your life if you tell me your Secret." For all things which lost their Secrets became somehow Less – less lucky, less canny, less curious, less wild. Less themselves, and a little more belonging to Death.

And whoever said Death was not lazy?

But the Queen only smiled and stretched so the stardust aurora sparked and popped along her spine. "I will tell you *your* Secret," she said when she had finished. "If you've courage enough to hear it."

And at that, Death was taken aback, and not a little worried. It had no notion which of its treasured Secrets she might have stolen, let alone how she'd managed it, and it greatly feared growing Less in any way. It was that worry that stopped Death leaping upon the little Queen and devouring her at once.

"Thief! You have no Secret of mine!" it shouted. Then, "Tell me at once!"

"I am no thief," she purred into the startled dark. "I found this secret on the corpse of a Sun you have never seen, but it is true as teeth and talons; you are not the only Death there is," she purred. "And I have bested bigger of your kind."

And with that, she turned herself inside out, as starlight's wont to do, pierced the whelming darkness like a razor, and slipped sidelong through the crack. A shocked thunder slapped the face of the air in her wake, and then with an outraged gasp the night began to rage.

Picture a young woman now, my dear, trembling reedlike in the storm as she whispers to the darkness at the campfire's twilit edge. With her face swaddled against the blowing sand, she breathes her only secret into the great Beast's rage. "I have not bled in too long," she says, and hopes the hot, red words – or perhaps those of her kindred, nearby and likewise whispering – might be enough to sate it.

"Not since just before the tribes gathered at the oasis of the black goat rock," she says. "Not since I danced in my green robes

141

for the elders, and again without them for the one who's smile shone so brightly." Eyes closed against the sand, how easy to remember that smile, but much harder now, for it to warm her as it had then. "But I do not know if my mother will smile at me when I give her another child to feed before winter." One hand curls around her little belly, the other gripping robes, veil and cowl tight over her thundering heart as she gathered up her courage to beg. To beg, though all knew there was no pity in Death. "Even so, please do not take him away, this little one. Not so soon as this. Not before I know his laugh, and hear him speak his name-!"

She stops, breath caught between a scream, and a gritty linen choke, for something – neither sand nor serpent, – has just curled past her leg. How her mind whirls with terrible endings! How she rushes back to the beleaguered fire's glow, back to where Death's claws may perhaps not quite reach. But first she trips, this light-footed one who danced for the elders – trips and tangles and sprawls out flat on the sand.

Heart pounding like drum skin in her throat, the girl shakes loose her robes, and from the whipping snarls tumbles a creature the like of which she has never seen. A little like a panther in flat, broad silver head and prickling whiskers, only it does not scream or leap upon her; a little like a jackal in the pointed ears tucked down flat against the skull, save that it has not snarled and lunged for her throat; a little like a wolf in the jagged smoke-ridge spine, and waterweed fluff of tail, save that it voices no bone-rattling howl to summon its hungry kin.

And in the slitted green eyes of the beast, the girl glimpses equal parts serpent, sun, and sleight. And perhaps, had her Secret fallen to Death's greed, had she become Less for the losing of it, our girl might have screamed again – screamed and kicked and fled to the fire. But as it has not, she spies out another mystery welling up within that lantern gleam, and it holds her enchanted.

The strangeling creature is our little Queen, of course; rumpled and vexed at the indignities of clumsy foot and tangling robes, but a better sight than the yawning maw of Death the dancing girl had expected. Uncertain, leery of disturbing the muted, offerings of her tribe, the girl gathers her courage and offers her hand to the strange little beast.

Who sniffs those painted fingers with suspicion due an interstellar intelligence who's outwitted a young, rash Death only to find her tail trodden by mortal toes. Then, because she was ever the forgiving sort, and because the Fire seems hard done-by in Death's blowing tantrum, the silvery Queen rubs her head along the girl's palm, and purrs a note of absolution. The girl scratches just *there*, behind the ear that's been buzzing ever since Death shouted in it, and the Queen leans in hard, closing her eyes for a moment of pure bliss. But then she leaps away, shaking dust and starlight from her fur, and goes to tell the struggling Fire the Secret of burning as Suns do, for the burning alone, though air and fuel there is none to be had.    She thinks the poor thing could use it.


Thus the tribe lived through the storm, though they never knew just how. The dancing girl suspected, and made a nest of her fine green robes for the silver Queen. And our Queen, intrigued by this folk so clever and so helpless at once, traveled on with the tribe, growing fat and round with desert mice, proffered tidbits, and of course, on Secrets.

For she was ever close when the tribe would venture to the gloom to whisper their accustomed sacrifices, with clever ears to catch them, ken them, and hold them fast in her knowing. And with each one she whisked away, the Queen felt the life of the Secret quicken inside her growing belly. And she curled up round and bright and tight in her nest of green linen, and she purred as she did when well stroked and well fed. But later, when the camp was a muted tapestry of sleepy breath and wheedling snores, she would slip from ear to ear and whisper those same Secrets back to their owners.

And so her tribe did *not* become Less. And that vexed greedy Death terribly, you may be certain.

In time, of course, the silver Queen brought forth those Secrets again; blind and mewling at first, but each one precious, seedling-wise, and hungry to learn the ways of the world-jewel they trod for home. They were not born quite so full of Knowing as their dam, but they were made all of Secrets, cunning, and hope, and in the Death-stalked opal world, there were few things quite so clever to be found.

They learnt the keeping of Secrets, they learnt the sidelong leap of light 'round corners, they learnt the sleeping tongue of men, and the way of seeing past the shape of a thing, to ken the Truth of it beneath. And too, they learnt the Lesser men's fear, which for them, meant violence, and so learnt to keep clear of those who had sold their Greater away in fear of Death.

And as the Queen's chosen tribe was a wandering band whose road cross-knit with many others', her get spread quicker than seed-fluff across the desert and beyond. The kits came fast and furry, and all did need to eat. Their mother sent them forth to travel whenever tribe met tribe, with a sizzling kiss to the flat of their heads, and a face-press hug of warning to be bold, be quick, and to watch the tricksy twilight close.

Soon enough, wherever Death found men gathered in Firelight, it also found lantern eyes watching from the gloom; found sleek, slippery spies *listening* when humankind gave up its Secrets in the vain hope of mercy; tickling whiskers giving those Secrets back to them in smug-rumbling purrs. And two may keep a Secret indeed, but not if one is Death, wasting what remains of the other into bone and skin and twitching, sleepless eyes. Those Secrets do not keep for long at all once the heart gives out.

Death began to wonder, eventually, if cats might not do better for its hoard.

But cats are hard to catch, as any who has tried soon learns, and harder still to kill. They know in their bones the Secrets of luck and leap, twist and tickle, fold, flicker, spindle, sprint and miracles the keenest eye cannot follow. They know these things at birth, just as they know their names, and the meat of the Secret that gives their coat its color.

What color, my sweet? Why can you not see the scorched blush of a Shame at face, tail and foot? The gingered, ruddy haunch of a Hatred? Icy white whiskers of a Terror? Misty grey of a soft Despair? Or the gleaming, golden flank of a Love? And the black cats wear their secrets too, but slyly, velvet silence spread like the void around the inevitable spark of their Secret. Do those who guess it gain a Knowing beyond their sisters? Many witches have believed it – and many black cats have encouraged that supposition, too. Find a black cat and ask. Its answer might startle you.

But yes, dearest one; cats know from birth just who they are, and what they ought to do. Even those who traveled far from the Queen's sight still dowsed their mother's distant love in their bones, buzzing with contentment and the old Sun's ghostly memories, their birthright. Who would not purr as well?

The chosen people built up cities in time; learnt the Secrets of quoin, ashlars and arch, of keystone and capstone and level and plumb, and they raised them up monuments not even Death's temper could knock down. Perhaps their canny cats taught them this, the legacy of all a dying star once did know. Or perhaps the cats just made sure the Knowing of these things, once they came to the tribes of men, did not slip away into the darkness' greedy ears. And perhaps *that* was why on some certain nights, all cats, grey in the darkness, blurred and purred together.

And when that rumbling, futtering, smugly fluttering sound filled up the empty night with hope – for which Death had neither taste, nor use, -- Death swore it would tolerate no more! No more of pillars and avenues. No more of brick and mortar, and city walls with Fire hid safe in lantern glass. No more of oil burned to the wick, houses snug against the storm, and hearth-tamed threshold hounds. No more of men who knew no taste of terror, or spell weaving, luck healing women, tickling loose Death's grip on their kin.

In a rage, Death left the third world, the shining sphere of beryl-and-pearl, and went to find the King. It packed its dark bulk as solid and tight as it could go, into the shadow of the closest treasure to the King, and there it growled in the voice of Tigers. "I have heard that Suns may die."

"Suns may do all things, I suppose," the young King answered, attention fixed on the architecture of his game. "Even if they do not know that they know. I am not surprised." He rolled a bit of dust into a ball beside a distant little treasure, and sent it carefully spinning. "What is this dying you speak of, and how is it done?"

Clenched tight in its pocket of shadow, Death was cramped and uncomfortably hot, and beginning to doubt its plan, but it pressed along all the same. "To cease; to stop; to burn no more," it guessed, and knew from the echoing ghosts of his stolen Secrets that the guess was pretty much correct. "To spin your toys loose into cold and silence, and care no more which dances more brightly; to taste of nothing, to Know nothing, to forget, and be forgotten. This is what dying is. And I am that which will bring the dying upon you!"

The young King thought about this. Within his roaring light, a knelling whisper of *'yes, this could just be truth,'* arose, unsettling and vexing at once. "I should prefer you did not," he said, and finally peered about for the source of the voice. "For

146

then I should have to fight you." He did not say that he should prefer not to have to fight anyone at all, of course, for he was a Sun, and not entirely a fool. Only he had just added several delicate moons to the pavane of his two biggest treasures, and he worried for their precision should he split his attention for warmaking.

"Suns die all the same," the voice went on, growing more and more sure of itself. "Think you that other doomed stars have not fought in vain?"

The Sun considered. Then, "I think you lie, voice in the darkness." The Sun lied himself. As any who've seen the promise of shimmering water, or far, delicate cities where no cities stand can witness, the Sun is an excellent liar. "I think you sow deception, and hide your true intent, and so I will not trust you."

"And if I bring you proof?" asked Death, beginning to smolder in his lessening shelter as the King's attention drew in. "There is a creature I have seen, who has the Death of Suns caught in her fur, who peers, as stars do, with light where darkness ought to linger. A thieving thing, all silver and guile, but witness to this dying I bring."

"And where is this creature?" asked the King, heedless as his tiny, golden world began to boil. "If such a creature exists within my sphere, I should have the knowing of it!" Ahh, how sad a thing that even Kings aloft in the Heavens may be led astray by pride.

"Just there," Death jackal-yelped, "on the third world, nacreous with life. Just there, where the sands lie smooth and long, and the green river floods the delta with mud. There, where gold gleams from atop bold and bothersome mountains. Look for her where the mud is carved into awful green rows, and shunts steal life from the great brown flow! Look for her there, and you will see!"

147

And the King, with eyes fiercer than any falcon, did look there. And he did find her, sleeping all in a blaze on the paw of a great stone creature (that was not unlike herself, a little) which guarded three mountains no earth-shift had ever raised. Her caravan had come to the place for trade with the settled folk, you see, and it amused the Queen to doze where Secrets gathered.

The yellow King saw the little Queen, bulging full with life, her flanks sound and round as starlight, her paws neatly tucked, her silken comet's tail curled over her toes like pearl haze over mountains. The Sun saw her, this child of Death and Secrets, this fierce little mother-creature asleep in the golden sands, and forgot all at once what it might be to die, for suddenly he knew what it was to Love.

Ahh, shall I tell you how he wooed her? Shall I tell you what songs he sang in his mighty voice? How all his dancing worlds took up in harmony, and improvised extra flourishes of joy? Shall I tell you of their whispered flirtations, their glancing seductions? And shall I tell you how gleeful Death became when it saw the silver Queen grow careless and in love? Oh no, there are a dozen tales and more to braid out of that great tangle of love and betrayal – tales that have found their way into the knowing of all men's stories, though the details change with the tongue that tells it.

What matters, is that Death *did* come upon the silver Queen one unwary night. That he did catch her up in his great claws, and he did gobble her down – yes, and all the squirming kittens inside her in a single gulp! But there he made his error, for even as black maw flexed around her, our Queen gave that sidelong leap, that spinning flicker of inside from out, and she leapt away with all the strength of her wiry satin feet.

And oh, how the thunder crashed in Death's throat! How it roared and belled, and shattered the great beast into a million pieces, each no bigger than a mouse on the sands! And how those stunned and terrified pieces of death did scatter when the children of the silver Queen, summoned from all roads and all firesides and all stone and timber cities by her startled cry, did fall upon them with lantern eyes and steely claws and quickly crunching teeth!

And it might have been a victory complete, but for this; the little silver Queen had missed her mark when she leapt for safety. And now she found herself aloft in the sky – too far from her tribe of men to shepherd their Secrets, too far from her get to rumble their bones with adoration – she was far, and far, and far beyond the reach of campfire dances, green linen nests, warm stone paws, quick desert mice, and treats smuggled off the table.

Perhaps the Sun, her lover, had caught the Queen's flight, curbed her careening tumble, and set her carefully to circle the world of opal she had so loved – so that she might always see it, and he might always see her. Or perhaps it was the opal world herself who caught the Queen at just *that* point in the sky, so round and sound and full of Secrets, that she could not but gleam with the young King's love, and light the darkness Death no longer ruled.

Or perhaps it was only luck.

But one thing is certain; when her children looked up from their feast of fleeting death, and let tiny shards slip chittering from between their claws – when they realized that she was gone, oh, how they mourned their mother's loss!

They cried for her. They called for her! They yowled with all anguish the Secrets of which they had been born, trying in the only way they knew, to bridge her back from that cold, far distance. Can you imagine such a sound, darling? Can you picture the dreadful screaming threaded through with great and awful Truths that no man or woman or child thought ever to hear from living lips? Can you imagine those thousands of anguished lungs singing Secrets aloud in panoply to the night that, while no longer occluded with Death, was still dark and wide, and full of listening ears?

Can you imagine the fear, the rage in the tribes who heard? How quick they must have taken up their killing tools, their slings, their clubs, their scythes and swords to silence those woeful, bristling tongues. The Queen, from her vantage saw, and she knew in her bones that Death might yet silence her legacy – coming now on flat, fearful human feet. But one last trick had she to play, for the Death of the old Sun had gifted her one Secret, which she had kept only for herself.

It was the Secret of confusion, of forgetting, and of muddling sense into noise and dazzle, and she worked it not upon her children, but upon the rising tribes of men. She wove the airless song of space tightly around their blunt ears, so that to them, the anguished song became a clamoring nonsense. She took from Mankind the language of Secrets, and grieved the theft from her airless orbit.

And so you know, Sweetling, how it is that the lithe moon grows so very full, then thin again as the weeks pass by – it is Secrets that fill her belly up there. The Secrets of her lover, and of his treasures, and of what she sees up there so far above the world. And where do you suppose those Secrets come once they are born? Why, do they not come here, Dearest, to her favorite opal world? And do they not whisper, tickling quick to the dreaming ears of poets, philosophers, mathematicians, architects, witches, and babes, who may not fully understand what they dream, but at least retain the starlit hint in their eyes when they waken?

And so now you know, Beloved, why it is that cats stalk shadows, hunt unseen murmurs, and pounce and gobble quick nothings that leave neither fur nor smudge nor naked tail upon the rug. And why, at twilight, they are at their quickest, their wildest, their most lissome and ferocious – for when else do the shadows meet and whisper and plan revenge? And you know too, why always there are some few too fiercely free to heed the wards of door and window, too mad and sidelong to allow a kindly cage of

150

man, even though they love the hand they dodge and the hearth they leave behind.  The pull of their Secret drives them like the tide, a throbbing in their bones.  They cannot but obey.

And perhaps you now guess why some hate cats, and others love them, and a little of why neither sort ever gives adequate explanation of it to the other.  It is their Secrets, of course, which decide the matter, but they, poor things, have lost both the Knowing and the words to speak to it.

And what is this?  What promised Truth have I forgot to tell you?  What sweetmeat held back unfair?  Ah, yes...

The reason cats do not weep is this:  The Moon, their mother, reached down her light to caress their woeful faces.  She dried their tears to soot-streak and starshine and whispered, tidelong to their bones that she loved them still.  And to this day, the marks remain – the fingerpad smears of the Mother's comfort sketched in glimmering fur across tiny faces in cozy litters, no matter the color and pattern of sire and dam.

Like random benedictions, these tiny tiger-faces come, and when they are seen, all other cats smile in secret, knowing they are yet beloved of the Moon.

And that there is no need to weep.

# A Momentary Interruption

Wait.
Wait, please -
I didn't catch what you were saying just now.
I'm sorry, so sorry.
But while you were speaking, I was listening to a louder sound -
I'm not sure how you could have missed it, -
But to me, it sounded like
A hundred hard-won peace treaties bursting into flames;
The crash of apologies, a thousand or less, hurled into the fireback;
Soft words a decade deep, unraveling;
Thread-snagged and fraying on jutting spars of charity and
politesse
As fifteen years of trust breaks up and falls away in
One.
Great.
Go.

And so I was listening to try and hear what kind of sound
All of that would make when it hit bottom.
I thought it might be a great, heaving splash, as into a sea of tears
or bile.
But a case could also be made for a ringing slap and gurgle,
As into La Brea's millennium of grudging decay,
Where, under pressure and a lifetime's aching,
It might someday fuel something smelly
And very loud.
All things considered, though, it seemed most likely to hit
With the sound of an off-colour Acme fanfare;
An anvil-and-mass-driver chorus, fit to crack a brittle desert floor
clear down
To where the Devil drinks Jack on Superbowl Sunday.
And that's why I didn't properly hear
Just what it was that you called me.

I wasn't far off, by the way, about the sound;
The end sounded rather like a grand piano,
Sleek as night and promises,
Its bones all heartbreaking beauty, elegance, and the lifelong passion
Of a man with songwood and steel in his veins;
Its finish sequin-buffed and satin-shined; dressed for the Ball
And trailing in its heart the fragrant ghosts of cigarettes, cheap booze, and broken faith,
Or something just as beautiful, just as tragic,
That was kicked carelessly, or spitefully, from the fifteenth floor,
Down to the unsurprised pavement below.
It caught only one small woman on the ground -
Pinned her mute and horrified in its growing shadow as it came
Crashing down.

And that's why I laughed.
Not at you, per se, but in wonder
That she hadn't thought to walk away,
Or even to run, while there was still time
To escape all that clanging, farcical destruction.
And perhaps, a bit, in appalled sympathy for how it must feel
To be hit in the face by fifteen years' worth of plummeting respect.

So do go on, please.
I'm sure my balance will have adjusted
By the time you've had your say.

# White Shoulder

First, put your thumb out.

It's not actually necessary of course; all you really need to do is
walk these days. Walk beside the highway, and don't be covered
in blood, and it'll only be a matter of time before one of them
swings over into your world. But like I say, the thumb is
traditional.

Always be sure it's not over the line though -- never cross the
Yellow unless you're stepping into steel. It's not safe. It's not
sane. You don't want to know the things that hunt your kind as
prey on the straightaway, little girl. And anyway, you'll ruin your
shoes. They've got to last you a long time -- as long as your own
name, you know, so see you treat them with care.

But don't watch your feet when you walk, and don't shuffle. That
draws the wrong sort. No, you watch the horizon, is what you do,
with a glance behind 'bout every fifty yards or so. More, if traffic's
thick. It's the glances that'll catch the right ones. A quick flash of
your face in their headlights, not even clear enough to see the
colour of your eyes, but it'll do, because then they'll have *seen* you.
They'll have pierced through the grey dust world for all of a living
heartbeat, and taken you in as more than a dingy blur on the
roadside.

And even if they don't stop that night, it still means they're yours.
Because they'll wonder, and they'll think about you, and they'll ask.
And when they hear your name and your story in some cozy place
that doesn't smell of asphalt and blood, they'll shiver. And they'll
tell how they glimpsed you beside the road when there was no
moon. And they'll look out for you every time they drive that road,

just hoping to see someone pale, sad and determined in the rain; something magical and white in their grey flannel world.

And on the night they can't drive on past anymore, they'll cross the Yellow for you. Even knowing what you are, where you're going, and how long you've been walking to get there, they'll stop, they'll lower the glass, and ask if they can take you home.

And that's when you can stop walking, honey.

# Hoarding

You must not pity me.
Truly.
Truly.


I am not one of those golden haired, spindleprick girls, you know.
I am wise to the dangers of cursed woods, fairy wells and
enchanted gardens,
Stepmothers, pastry architecture, and gifts from odd-eyed old
women.
Nor have I failed to heed advice from talking beasts or furniture.
My mother is my own blood kin,
My father lives, and loves me,
And I got on with my sisters as well as ever sisters do.


So let us have no sympathy for the middle child of the Woodcutter
King,
Brown-haired daughter of that lucky Jack who plucked kingdom
and bride alike
From the crown of a white glass hill.
If we, his daughters cannot be so lucky, so plucky, and so well
equipped
With magical maille and apples of gold, well… it is not beyond
understanding;
We are none of us third sons of forest peasantry, after all.


But if you must pity, do not pity me, for I do not wish it.
No clucking tongues, no shed for the Princess
Who was neither eldest and Heir, nor youngest and Most Lovely.
Save sympathy for little Aramista, plucked from her roses by a
passing ogre.
He did not care that she was the darling of Court and Queen,
Only that she looked golden and sweet,

If a little skinny.
Save sorrow for serene Kitaria, shouldering the passionless weight
Of a marriage of state;
Nary a handsome Jack, nor plucky Jane to prick the heart,
Bestir the ivory breast, or singe the royal lineage with tinder-spark
unbidden.
But do not pity me my lot, for it was of my own making.
My fault.
Entirely.
Entirely.


Stories will later tell, I suppose, that the Dragon stole me away;
Caught me from my horse at hunt,
Plucked me from a royal parade,
Or ravaged the land until I was surrendered up to him;
A canapé in coronet; a royal nonpareil;
A pretty, sticky toffee in satin slippers to bait the quest for a better
class of Jack
Than will come to slay a marauder of livestock alone.
Or perhaps they will say that my mother
(Who will surely become Stepmother for the crime,)
Grew jealous of my beauty and summoned the Dragon to carry me
away.
And we may, for drama's sake, scatter a silver comb, mirror shards,
Needles and silk thread about my tower room,
For proper princesses, you know, sit just so,
And make tiny, perfect stitches out of all their sunny days.


They do not ride to hunt with their father and brothers, these
proper princesses;
Do not ford streams and jump bramble hedges
With legs astride and wild hair flying;
Do not turn aside from the belling pack to seek out

The pitiful groan of a beast unseen;
Do not venture shattered saplings, and scorch-curled ferns
Seeking after groans and sighs.
And never, these golden ball girls,
Upon finding a Dragon felled in the new-made clearing
Would tear their linen hems to bind its wounds
(Some sword's edge straight, others spear's thrust deep.)
Oh no, they do not ease the bat-span vermillion wing
From the pinewood tangle while their panicked palfrey pulls loose
its tether
And drums a fleeing tattoo through the woods.
And they do not, these prized and precious girls,
Most certainly do not fetch stream water,
Diamond–cold in soft royal hands,
And help the poor thing drink.


I did those things.
I freed the Dragon from the wreckage of his fall.
I burnt my hands on his blood.
I soothed his great, fretting head across my knees,
Though his horns bruised my ribs.
I stood for my Dragon's life when the huntsmen found my ranging
horse,
And tracked her back to where we hid.
T'was I who sent them off, never seeing what lay in the new-
crushed dell.
They bowed to my will.
Mine, child of the Woodcutter King,
(And no less brave or clever, I decided, for want of a magical
stallion.)
They went, the beast unseen,
And until his sky bright eyes opened in awareness, I stayed.

A Dragon's great size, his scales and wings and fiery breath
Do not banish him to far off caves and wastelands, it seems,
Nor does his hoard come creeping coin by coin,
Like gleaming mice on tiny, shiny feet.
I'd hardly thought, before, what magic
Might draw hoard and hoarder together.
(Dragons are rarer than Ogres and Hags, after all,
And a Princess must have priorities.)

A Dragon may go shod and shaven, it seems, at need,
And bring his might in manly form to mine or market hall,
Or wherever there are shining things to be got.
Fierce in finance they are, canny in commerce, tireless at trade;
Men at the barrelhead would blench to know the hand they've
shaken
Will, betimes, turn iron clawed and scaled from end to end,
And that their cool coin will mound up high in a far, forgotten
cavern
And heated scales will press it palm-close and cozy for decades,
Or until some thieving Jack comes sniffing.

This, I did not know when I turned my father's men aside.
This, I did not learn until the Dragon rose before me,
Broad and bronze in the dappled shade, with a Jack's rakish grin
And nary a fang or scale to be seen;
So beautiful, he was, so daring and darling that my heart caught
fast in his golden hair
And could not struggle free.
I had saved him, thinking I did not care to see such majesty fallen
low
And pitiful with pain,
Not when it was in my power to charm him, to tame him,
To bring this mighty creature into my debt,

159

For this is how such things are done, as any child knows
And Princesses better than most.


I had not known he would be beautiful,
Or what a weighty thing his gratitude would be.
And he *was* grateful, this you must understand.
My Dragon, so fiercely bright the thought of his eyes scorched
hidden places,
He was grateful to me,
He was fond of me,
He was smitten,
And he courted with all the passionate ferocity of a midwinter
dream
(When snow and silence make all folk mad, a little.)
Oh, but imagine it if you can –
Fine, diamond ferocity, intense as molten gold,
A blazing desire spent not upon rubies, platinum, pearls,
Jade, ivory, emeralds or any gleaming thing,
But trained instead, upon a girl's tender heart.
Might not even a Jack's canny daughter,
(Too wise to nibble at gingerbread houses,)
Catch fire and blaze under such regard?


Stop that smile, sly one.  Swallow that sniggering jest.
This ballad runs not to barnyard or barrack room.
It is not to be sung, ale in fist when the tavern night winds down to
farts and foolishness.
Make your own stories cheap if you will, but never mine
Never my love –
Not when the cost has been so very, very great.


My lover's eyes were hot as gasflame or cloudless July,
His hair all gold when the sun seduced its curls,

His teeth pearl-smooth and flashing
At my smallest joke, my simplest question, my merest glance
betimes.
Oh, he charmed us all, from Chatelaine to chambermaid.
This hapless Lord, of gentle speech and manner --
Beset by robbers in a country not his own,
and rescued by the Princess' own kind hand --
The story alone was enough.
Tongues wagged wild at Court,
And many hearts made a futile racket beneath their silk and stays.
My Lover played his part well.
He offered the doubtful nothing to fear,
The fearful nothing to doubt,
Was all charm and generosity, regardless of rank or connection.
But it was for me that his eyes burned hottest,
And I knew to the depths of my clever heart that he loved me
As no other had ever known love.

And yes, he did love me, of that I am sure.
And there is nothing in that to pity.
Nothing.
Nothing.

## II

Of course we could not stay.
How could his vast appetites,
Enough to feed his great and hidden fire,
Go unnoticed, himself so trim and fine?
How could his perfection weather jealous scrutiny for long?
He feared for me, most of all, he said.
He breathed his concerns into the tender space behind my ear,

Whispered of our enemies within the court;
Of ambitious men who saw me as chattel,
The engine of their ascent.
He told me that Kings marked wealth not in armies, gold, or
knowledge,
But the power that wound about their daughters' unwed hands,
Ring-bound and sold to distant, powerful Princes.
(For all the good Jacks come to their crowns through valor, of
course,
And are not born in palaces,
Combed sleek by slaves at whom they throw their hunting boots,
And promised genteel brides with bright-bruising skin as their
right of birth.)
I thought of loveless Kitaria, and I trembled.
I thought of my father's Seneschal, Generals, Advisors,
How they watched me as grocers watch their plums,
Gorgon-grim lest the fruit be bruised before it is bought,
And I knew we could not stay where my rank
Might see me sold away from him who loved me
So fiercely,
So dearly,
So well.

And yet, though he was mine, and I was his
He was not Mine; was no fit man, however charming or rich,
To claim a Princess' hand, unknown as he was to any Court,
His lands and title a feline fiction.
Nor was I His, for our Kingdom faced no Witch Queen's curse,
Ogreish army, Faerie spite, or Bears.
Not even a plague of bored Brownies wrinkled the stultified peace,
And had I a golden ball to lose, with him lurking at well's bottom...
Well.
There are some tricks may only be played the once.

And so he could not ask for my hand.
But I, oh I could offer it.
And so I did.
And so he took it,
And all the rest of me alongside.

And so you must not pity me, for I have flown.
I have seen the patchwork earth in fire-pricked velvet flow;
Have smelt wind so pure, so wild it had no word for sweat or
smoke or tears;
Have shivered in awe so cold and wide,
Not even my lover's blaze could warm it full away.
When darkness pressed us close in the earth-smelling damp,
I shivered against his scales, as stiff and cold as the gold beneath
my back,
And my dreams brimmed full of empty sky,
And tiny fires, too small, too far below to warm me.

It was not that he turned cold; I know this.
How could he chill, brimful of fire and sunlight,
This beast of flame, seething with passions
The Courtly Dance had long denied?
If it seemed cold in the high, lonely mountains, then surely it was
me --
Hearth-pet Princess that I was,
A silly, spoilt girl,
Vain enough to think the empyrean reach might welcome me
unchallenged,
And set me down unchanged from how I had gone aloft.
I had so very much to learn.
He had so very much to teach me
Once the spoils of Court were fallen far behind us,
Once the mountains reared high

To wall the kindly sky in silence, stone and snow.

I learnt first of satin slippers, broidered o'er with glass and silver;
Quite unfit for cave-dark wanderings,
Half lit with candle flame or distant sun.
Caves are dangerous places,
Where slanting drifts of coin and sharp-edged crystal may slither
From beneath doeskin soles,
And pitch one headlong into pool or pillar, or spur of heartless
stone
At the merest nudge of wing, or dreaming tail-thrash.
T'was luck that only he could see my motley skin,
Marked worse than lentil-mattresses could do.
He forgave the bruises, laughed fondly, ruffled my hair with
brimstone breath,
And called me clumsy duckling, precious, and his fawn.
Then he took the slippers, would have burnt them to glittering ash,
Heeding no protest of mine;
No matter that my mother had made them just for me
To match my sixteenth birthday ballgown,
'They had betrayed their mistress,' he said.
They had done me harm,
And he would tolerate no harm to what was his.
And was I not his?
Save that the shoes were fairy-blessed, and valuable,
That turned his wrath aside,
Just enough to spare that pair, alone out of them all.

But he was right, you know,
For bare-shod, I soon learnt the way of creeping,
Mouse-quiet past his bed
(He slept so light, so wary, as owners of great hoards must sleep.)
And I learnt to go soft, bestirring neither coin nor cup,

Nor tripping over bones in the darkness.
And if the rocky path outside was unforgiving to my feet,
Well.
What need had I to venture far from my lover's lair?
What need had I to walk out, and seek the coarse company
Of plotting, greedy mountain peasants;
Witches' girls,
Woodcutter's sons,
And such grim, suspicious folk as may be found in uncouth places
Where Dragons haunt the sky?

What use had I for riding boots when I could keep no horse
From my bright lover's appetite?
What use had I for broghans when the mountain's peak
Bore no fit soil for gardens,
Gave root to neither flower nor tree
Beyond a few grudging thistles clinging sour and stubborn to the
stone?
And what need had I for fine gowns or jewels with no Courtiers to
see?
My lover thought me fairer unadorned,
He assured me,
And, he said, I would most likely lose them in the dark,
Shred their hems on jutting stone,
Smirch silk with soot, drench velvet in the cavern pool,
Than care for such beautiful things as they deserved.
He was an expert, you see, in beautiful things;
He never misplaced the slightest tin plate or crystal chip,
And knew by touch the minting mark of every coin upon his
mounded bed.
Better that he should take my treasures on,
Calculate my pearls and combs into the tally
That swirled and sparked beneath his horns, and keep them

Somewhere they would be safe,
Forever.

He brought me plainer clothes;
Dun and homespun, loose at waist, looser at bosom,
Smelling just a little like chamomile soap, rye flour, children and
despair.
Such garb the like of which I would not ruin
In the sooty, metal-edged gloom where he made our home.

Where we made our home.
I meant to say we.
I did.


### III

It was in such mean attire that I first saw the stranger,
Wandering unwary through high meadows the locals knew to fear.
From this I knew him, as much as by his robes, pack mule and
tonsure,
To be dangerous beyond measure.
Prying shepherds may go missing in the lonely heights;
Meddling maidens may fail to return from their flower- and gossip-
gatherings;
And thieving Jacks who come sniffing after treasure
Do not always return to collect their tavern bragging rights.
These things will happen in wild places.
But a priest,
A man of name and letters, not given to fictions or fancies;
Who goes nowhere he does not mean to go,
And is expected at his road's end;
Here was a man, for all his temperate face and humble mien,
Brimful of peril.

I fled him,

Fast as I could with the slithering scree chewing at my toes,

And my heart fluttered, a trapped bird in a stranger's woolen stays.

He would not leave his mule and pack, I thought,

Surely he would follow the goat-thin track downward

To a terse village welcome, and a dust-clung church.

They wanted a savior like him,

A holy foil to the devil of whom they had learnt not to speak too loud,

Lest his wings eclipse their sun forever.


No,

I did not think the young priest would follow me.

I did not guess he had seen my hair unbound in the sun,

A banner of cinnamon silk against the sky.

I did not guess that compassionate concern, or damnable curiousity

Would spur him to the chase like a braying Hound of God.

An awful rattling we made upon the mountainside,

Enough to wake the weariest Wyrm from slumber.

Had my Love been home, not ranged afar in service to his gold,

That Priest in his cursed sandals,

Could never have caught me,

Brought me to bay at the very gate of home,

Shocked me colder than stone with my own name,

Shouted out in the aching tones of home;

The long-lost cant of warm valleys, orchards, and sunlight fields

With no more peril than transfigured frogs in muddy pools

And an Ogre or two.


No Hag's curse could have caught me tighter.


I begged him to go.

I told him it was not safe for the likes of him so far aloft,
That the treeline was the end of Man's territory,
And above it, were Monsters.
He would not go.
I would have said it was no safer for me,
Should the Dragon scent a stranger's breath upon his threshold.
He was chivalrous, after a priestly fashion, and he would have
gone, I'm sure,
Only...

Only he offered me bread; travel-hardened,
Crumbling, stale from weeks on the road.
Still, I had not seen its like in oh, so very long.
And I was so tired of meat,
(However freshly got and hot, its bloody, rank thud upon the stone
Always made me flinch,
Which always made the Dragon laugh.)
And dear God how could I dare to ask, with hunger gnawing at my
spine,
What kind of meat was this when it still had skin?
And did it know its name?
One bald haunch looks like another in a Dragon's eyes;
Fat drips and gristle pops the same in flame,
And I was not so spoilt as to turn up my once-delicate nose at his
generosity,
For long.
If my tender belly rebelled and would not settle,
I took care the Dragon never heard me retch --
He thought me too thin already.

So for the price of a lump of road biscuit, I betrayed my heart,
And let the stranger stay.
I let him speak of towns where my name was known,

My face sketched in song, my story told
(At least unto the question mark where all knowing of it ended.)
Places where they knew my Father sought any word of me;
That my brothers quested afar;
And one, who came west to the mountains, had never returned;
That my Mother dreamt me in peril;
Starving, cold, and trapped at the whims of a monster,
And wept for weeks;
That my Sister consulted with Witches for news.
I sat in that cold autumn sunlight,
Let him feed me bread and apples, sharp, hard cheese,
And the news of my Father's court.
I let him call me by my snug-fitting name,
Mother given, summer-warm, and garden-bright,
And sounding not at all like a smoke-huff grunt,
Like "Woman,"
Or "You.")
I tried not to think how long it had been
Since that name had suited me.


And then I sent him away, I swear I did.
He was a priest, a good man, an honest man,
Sworn to a God beyond any temptation a mere Princess,
Especially one bare shod, thin, grubby and wrapped in stolen
clothes could offer.
I did not offer.
He put not a toe inside the cavern's shadow,
Glimpsed not a golden glimmer within.
I told him no slandering lies,
Spun no tale of woe there in the bright sunshine.
However low I had fallen, a King's daughter had still some little
pride;
I did not wish him to know the depth and number of my failings.

One thing only did I give him, when he pleaded,
Insisted, and swore to return if I gave it not.
To ward him off, I relented, borrowed foolscap, ink, and a fine-
made pen
And wrote a note, one page in my long-unpracticed hand,
To tell my Father that I was well, and wished for nothing.

It was a mistake.
It was a disaster.
It was an act that would bring ruin, though I knew it not then.
How was I to know?  When had I gone out of the cavern's sight?
When had I ventured near as a stone's throw to the treeline,
Let alone the village, or any other town below it?
I thought he would take months to send it onward,
For winter would come sooner than any messenger, surely.
And in those months, he would, perhaps, misplace my note
Or forget why he ever wished to have it.
How could I know this Priest with his poky, thistle-full mule
Could send my note, spurred by rumors of reward, from the
mountain's flanks
To the Logger's river town, where barges fly swifter than birds,
surer than rumours,
Arrow-straight into the heart of the Woodcutter's Kingdom?
With the turning leaves, the damage was all done.

I knew only, at that time, that the Priest went his way soon after,
And that once his shadow was gone,
I swept every crumb from our doorstep
And scrubbed the stone with ash and cold grease
(Rancid-rank, but the best I could do by way of soap.)
And as I did, I prayed for that guileless Priest's sake,
That my deceit would be shelter enough for him,
And perhaps for me.

It was not.
But my prayer went not entirely unanswered,
For my Lover, when he read in the mule's tracks
The sign of an interloper so close to his hoard and home,
Took his accounting only unto me, and did not tear the village apart
In search of his imagined cuckhold.

Don't think I fail to see that pitying look.
Strike it from your eyes;
It was not so bad as all that.
I know him, you see?
I know his moods like a boatman knows his river
And the rapids might shake me bow and stern,
But I know how to hold on until the river calms.
Nor must you blame him, really,
For it is only that, for all his great power,
For all his might and towering flame,
My lover scares so very easily.
Sometimes he cannot help but rise to battle
Even when there is no foe to fight
But me.

I am all he has, you see?
There is only me to understand him,
Only me (and his bed of gold,) to love him,
Or to care.

IV

Autumn breathed its last in storms

That laced the mountain's knees in snow.
Churchbell echoes wandered through the trees,
And jangled off the high, bare rocks.
Smoke in the ringing air stank of iron and coke
And anvil-song
Though the village blacksmith was long since gone.
(Suspicious, the Dragon said,
Untrustworthy, with eyes too narrow and hands too big.)

I was alone that day; aloft in the storm,
Fancy-taken in my bare feet and cloak of fur,
(New-gifted, as I'd healed from that awful Autumn afternoon,)
To climb the dizzy heights and peer down
Down a-derry derry down.
To stare along the lonely wind,
The bending trees,
The mountain's knees,
And scry the distant river through the storm.
To stand in solemn silence with my head pressed hard to Heaven,
And think how might it be to have wings of my own,
And stepping from the stone, to spread them wide and fly
Or fall.
In such snow-soft pillowing clouds, either would do.
And oh, you mustn't look at me so,
You mustn't think me mad,
For I was terribly sane just then,
And I had learnt not to mind the cold so very much.

So it was that while I hugged the sky and thought of wings,
I glimpsed creeping steel through a break in the trees.
Through raveling flurry, shredding cloud and creaking evergreen
I saw them come;
Horses under torches, orange with ironlight;

Roan flanks, oil-dark hooves and smoke-puff, gusting breath at the burden of
Burnished steel and dark-boiled leather,
Such barding livery as only sees the eve of battle.
And knights as well.
I had seen such dreadful display before --
(Jacks will find Giants, as they say, and Dragons, Hags and Ogres much the same,)
I had learnt to run into darkness when Heroes came,
And hide myself behind the gold
(Better spoils, I knew, than I,)
Until the gory business was done, and only ash and echo-screams remained.
Then, summoned at length, emerge
To roll another shattered shell of Knightsteel clanging into the trees --
Mementos, lest the villagers take notions.

Oh yes, I had seen Jacks come in boots and shoes and brown bare feet,
But never in such numbers as these.
Never a company of steel, in bristling rank and file,
Never such horses crowding the high meadow with hide and haunch,
Never such streams of riding fire, like a serpent through the storm
Winding unerringly to my nest.

I was caught out;
No sheltering hoard to shield me.
They were nearer the cave, mounted,
And though storm-cloaked, I dared creep only so near,
For there was precious little cover by the cavern's mouth anymore.
I lurked just close enough to see the scouts,

Boldest of that gleaming company,
Halloo the monster's lair.
The name they called out had once been mine.
I crouched behind middling boulders and tried not to breathe
Or weep.
They would go.
They would surely go when they got no answer,
When they got no fight.
They would steal what they could carry, and they would ride away
And perhaps I would not have to see it
When my Lover tracked them down and claimed,
With ruddy interest, what was his.

But when the heroes clambered out again,
Their gauntlets brimmed, not with proper plunder,
But rather the fluttering waft of sunlight silk,
And delicate slippers, sewn with silver threads and glass.
A rosewood chest full of pretty trinkets
To make a Princess glitter and smile,
Once upon a time.
Only that, they stole:  only me,
Only the tokens I had left to show of the She who had been,
Carried off, now, in iron-hinged stranger's hands.
'For proof,' one of them hailed the rest, careless above the keening
wind,
'Here's proof she has been here.'

They did not stay after that.
The wind is fierce as flame, so high against the clouds,
And they were valley folk; broad and kind, and not fitted
To such grudging camps as this.
They went; a column of flame and steel
Tracing each curve of the long road downward --

The road I had never quite seen clear between the trees.
(Not that I had looked for it, of course.)
I saw it now as the serpent of men went their firelit way
And took the ghost of me along for hostage.

I hoped they would ride all night,
All week without resting.
I hoped they would ride forever and fly,
Home to the valley's bosom, and never more,
Not one of them, brave the haunted heights
In search of Lost Girls' slippers.

A scrap of silk, golden thread, fairy luck, glass beads;
A smudge of gilt on ivory heels in which a girl might dance, but
never run;
'A pittance,' I told myself
As they went their way, and the snow drank up their tracks,
He would not care.  What they'd taken had little value,
And anyway, was mine.
And so I slipped into my lover's bedchamber, struck myself a little
light,
And settled down to count.
Yes.
I was very much a fool.
I know that now.

Do they tell each other about us, I wonder?
Gather in ruddy caverns where all is gold and fury,
To rumble tales of we heartless ones who are so very cruel to
them?
Do they warn each other of Princesses' lies;
Honour-smirching, monster-making of the poor, trusting reptile
Who tried his best, kept her safe,

Gave her wealth, and fought all comers,
Only to find himself betrayed,
Deceived, his great heart trodden under little dancing feet?
And do the other Dragons nod and grumble
That we are all alike in grace, greed, and guile,
Wanting only the chance and choice moment to turn,
And to show ourselves false as fool's gold?
That we cannot be,
Not one, not even one of us, trusted?

Do the wise advise their jealous brothers,
(Hunched low over steaming cups of spite,
While they clean our hopes from between their teeth,
Spit our promises like cherry pits into the molten pool,
And drip occasional, unnoticed rubies from their hooked red
claws,)
That we Princesses must be shown
How fragile is our beauty, and how fickle the power it lends?
That, once we are not so proud and pretty anymore,
stripped of flashing smiles and courtly graces,
When not even our closest kin would know us,
And we are left with faces to make peasants spit
And ward 'gainst evil eye,
That only then are we fit companions?

Do they learn to treat us all this way?
Or was it only me?
Did I fail, somehow, to learn his every lesson,
So that it was by claw and flame I must be taught the betrayal
In lying letters to spying fathers,
Thieving knights lured to debauchery on my absent lover's bed,
Then sent their smirking way,
Taking each a token of my favors between them?

Need I have learned repentance through fire?

He did not mean me to die
Even in his flaming rage, he loved me too much, I am sure,
And could not bear to see another take me away --
Not even Death itself.
And so I lived; neither burnt to twistwood and gristle on the
melting gold,
Nor drowned face-down in the cavern pool
Where my dervish flailing sprawled to an end.

I remember no more, save that he who so loved me
That he could leave nothing of me for anyone else to love,
Did not once look back when he left me there
In hissing steam and ringing silence,
Alive.


V

Do not ask me how I stood, or when.
I cannot tell you by what means I walked or crawled,
Claw-fingered, stump-footed through the icy stays
That winter wrenched tight around the world.
I can only tell you that my next clear memory was of bells
And light through coloured glass,
And haunting hymnsong voices.

I could just see him through a swatch of Virgin blue;
His cup, his chaplet, his pile of bread before him at the altar,
His face turned toward heaven, alone amid the throng still
unafraid.
His voice was the loudest in that little house of God
His prayer so clear it cut me bloodless in the winter night,

And I could not go in.
For had I not known the flames of Hell?
And did I need a glass to see that my sins smouldered on my face
Where none could fail to read them?
I had danced to my destruction as surely as did Eve,
Or the Snow-Girl's mother.
There was no place there for me in that holy house,
And anyway...
The candle light hurt my eyes.
I took myself back to the square,
Where wind had driven the snow up deep as secrets,
And the houses did not so closely loom,
And there I surrendered
In snow as soft as clouds.
Once its kiss turned wet against my eyelids,
I thought I might open them to watch the moon
And wait.

And then I remember the crunch of wagon wheels.

And then I remember dreaming of my mother, singing a lullabye
while a mule brayed

And hooves rattled nearby.

And then I remember a ponderous sweep of pine branches, arching
like cathedral bones
Against an empyrean sky.

And then I remember a salty, greasy taste;
Bitter, like willowbark
Or tears.

And sometime after that, I woke,
Feeling as though I had slept for a hundred years.


The Witch had a permanent twist in her lip,
Lacy scars that knotted like rope from nose to ear.
An ironic, fraying end arched one eyebrow forever in disbelief.
The Witch had an eye as blue as deep water,
As wise as winter, and as merciful as spring.
Just the one;
A smooth green pebble held the other's place
And reflected no light at all.
The Witch had a hand curled up tight like a claw.
Somehow, despite the scars, it was not rough on my savaged skin,
But gentle as milk, scented with herbs and honey.
The Witch had no voice,
But she made herself plain without recourse to words;
A corvid croak, or cackling laugh, and all,
From her girl to her goat to her geese, to her guest, knew the
Witch's will.
A greenstone glare, and not one of us would disobey.
She did not often glare.
Rather she smiled, or as near as her scarred face would allow,
And how could I not remember, when her blue eye sparkled with
mirth
Or welled sympathy;
When she held me, shaking in nightmare's wake
As the winter nights ground on in towering silence,
Dreams of fire, and a welter of sodden sheets;
That all Witches begin their lives as Maidens?


She gave me herb salves and tea, and my weeping skin healed
Fast and sound as a fairy's blessing, though not so fair.
Not even magic could do that.

She gave me simple fare, the like of which makes peasants strong
And Princesses live, despite themselves.
She gave me gentle work to keep the idling, pitiful hours at bay.
And she gave no sign that my scars or silly tears,
My weak hands or numb-clumsy feet,
My flinching fear of wing-shadows in the sky,
Or my night-screaming upset her in the least.
She gave no sign of knowing I was ruined,
And seemed to think I only wanted patience, peace, and feeding
up.
Some days I nearly believed it myself.


Word came up the valley from time to time, of the Dragon,
My lover, my destroyer, my terrible mistake.
I could not always fail to hear the tales;
He was raiding openly along the rich riverlands of the Woodcutter
King,
Burning crop and croft, plucking sheep and peasant girls from the
fields,
And making war, now and then, with the bands of knights
Sent out to bring him down.
If he returned to the mountain,
If he looked for me in the slag-scorched cavern that had been our
home,
If he raged to find me not where he had left me,
I did not know it.
No fire scathed the forest, no belling panic rang from the village up
Or down the mountain's flanks,
And though the sound of rushing wind made me flinch and duck,
To escape the sky's broad blue stare,
I saw neither scale nor skin of my Dragon.
Only by tales did I know, secondhand,
That he lived at all.

Then one day it was not the miller,
Come to trade flour for a potion-cure,
Or the barge town midwife, or lamed logger
Who carried news of the Beast to the Witch's cothold,
But a knight -- weary-eyed and smirched with dust and soot and blood.
And there was nowhere I could run,
For soap was brewing on the hearth, and I was wanted lest it scorch,
And haunt the cottage with smoky nightmares.
And so I stayed when he came in,
Though through the open door I glimpsed his gear,
And recognized the blaze of sunny silk he'd bound to his lance-haft
By way of battleflag.
His pitying glance at my firenook corner made it plain though;
He knew not who had worn that gown last.

The beast no longer flew -- that was his news.
The scarlet wings were lance-tattered lace now,
And now the Dragon lay at bay in the ruins of a town
A day's ride down, between the mountain's toes.
Army-ringed, his bolt-hole, but thick with hostages the Crown,
He told us, looking down,
Did not care to spend.
He had been sent to ask, he said, for poison.

There followed long stifling silence, and then I realized
She was looking at me solemn and still,
As though we did not both know where, on her crowded shelves,
Just such a poison lay.
Her eyes, sweet and grave, fixed me in place --
The green no better clear than the blue, as she waited

181

For me to decide.

I did not see the knight riddle me out.
I only heard his ragged gasp,
And glimpsed, corner-eyed,
The firelight slide along his kneeling steel.
Palm to plated breast, shocked face tucked reverently low,
He coughed.
And dreading lest I hear him say 'your Highness',
I lunged up; fetched the black bottle quick as I could,
Thrust it out in my curled claws, and might have cried 'take it and
be gone!'
But the Witch, my savior, my friend, curled her warm claw over
mine,
Pressed my trembling shoulder still
And, smelling all of chamomile soap, rye flour, children and hope,
Whispered soft in my ear the first, the only word
I ever heard her say;
"Go."


VI


We rode the day in silence, this stranger and I,
Hemmed in with snowcrunch, armor's clank,
And a thousand wordless questions.
The Witch lent her mule and cart,
For I could not yet
(Nor, perhaps, ever again,)
Ride astride,
And would not bear the cradle of the stranger's arms and thighs,
However nobly intended.
Neither, it seems, found in the other's company

Any sort of comfort,
For every step and jostle ground out the silent questions,
Until the gristle and grief gave way to truth;
That somehow I had not seen my happy ending's sad decay –
Not until the end.
It had seemed, before, a gradual collapse of courtesy into disdain,
Into scorn, into disgust, into hatred, and murder
While I struggled in vain to please, to comfort, to understand just
how
I could wound my love so terribly that he must wound me back.

And what could I say of it to this polished messenger
With his innocent, outrage --
This questing Bravo, appalled and awkward in the shadow
Of the sunlight gown I had refused to put on again?
What answer could I make to those guileless eyes
Which had seen the blood of monsters,
But never the terrible grace of their loving?
What could I tell him of restless passion, reckless abandon,
And the awful joy of being utterly overwhelmed?
He could not understand.
I did not wish him to;
I would not smirch his honest shine with ash
Just because my own was scorched all away.

Nor did he ask, in all those mule-slow, downward hours,
'Why?'
Merely, 'was I weary, did I hunger, should we rest?'
I was.  I did.  But I could not bear to tarry,
For the wind flung greasy woodsmoke up the canyons
And scoured the sky with guilt.
Flame gouts rent the far darkness
And battle thunder shook even the stoical mule's nerve.

But on we rode, till the dawn-cracked sky bled, rose and gold
Across the sprawled and smoking wreck of the village
We had come to late to save.

The mule rebelled, not to be goaded onward,
And so the knight rode down alone to his peers,
Bruised survivors of the monster's midnight sally.
The Woodcutter's banner crowned a billowing smithy,
As singed and stubborn as the knights below,
And I might have wondered --
Did the Hero King rest beneath it?
Or did my brothers dress their lances thus
To brave the beast who had stolen me away?

I might have wondered.
Only there in the smoke and granite shatter
Of a tiny churchyard, lay the Dragon himself --
The crimson hulk on which I had wagered my heart
And lost,
And I was lost,
Lost all again.

My lover lay athwart the crumpled churchspire,
Twisted, limp and smoldering, much as I had seen him first.
Thicker, though, his thorny scales; darker, bristling now
With spear-hafts, arrows, swords.
Black, his claws, one horn sheared ragged,
His beard a crusted clump as he laid his head
In the lap of a shattered angel.
When had he grown into a monster?

Then, golden and rosy as the creeping dawn, I saw her;
A soft, silly girl with love skulking blue and foolish in her eyes.

She crept like a cat past the Quest of Knights whose fellows
Lay sundered in the Dragon's gory bed.
They knew he breathed, seethed yet with life,
And scented the dawn with sulfur, cinnamon,
And blood --
And they spared no glare for a simple girl
Wandering witless where she oughtn't.
And she, clever puss, gave no man cause to ask;
What had she in that basket beneath her cloak of riding red?
Where did she mean to go,
And with whom?

I left the mule cart,
Took my blackthorn stick and black glass bottle,
And rushed to catch the pretty fool before the Dragon.

She screamed a little, seeing me hunched and leering
Through ragged smoke at the churchyard gate,
Clutched her iron-crossed throat with one hand,
Her traveling bundle with the other.
I laughed, crow-cold, at her warding sign.
I told her to go while still she could go,
Then cackled again when she called me Witch,
Hag, Jealous Betrayer.
She swore to stand with him who loved her
As no other knew love.

Then I sketched a meaningless symbol
In the smoking air, and named it a curse
To turn her silly face, and all her children's besides,
Into that of an ass -- the better to reflect her wit
Should she put one foot inside the hallowground --
And she ran.

I would have run as well when I was her,
And had more fear of Hags than handsome Dragons.
Before I learnt how fearsome beauty could be.

And then where could I go, but down
Down a-derry derry down?
To stare along the foetid wind,
The tumbled graves,
The palisade,
And trace his flexing hulk athwart the steam.
To stand in solemn silence with my eyes fixed on Hell,
And to think how might it feel to have no heart of my own,
And pouring my small draught out, anoint his gaping wounds with
death
Or agony.
In such chill revenge, either would do.

My Witch-gifted boots scraped moss and soot,
Cryptstone, cindered pews, and dead men's shoes,
And so the Dragon heard me come.
He hailed me unseen in a brittle voice, like saplings
Split beneath a terrible weight – called soft a name not mine.
Her name, I reasoned, and did not answer.
Then the fickle wind reconsidered,
Unraveled the veil of ruined dreams between us,
Left us eye to startled eye across the broken angel's back.

"You," he said after long silence,
And his brimstone scorn burned my eyes to water.
"I might have known you'd come."
And then he smiled, smugly grotesque around a chainmail scrap,
One eye gone elf-shot hollow and vague.
And in my palm, the little bottle curled,

Weighty as all the world's evils.
It was fragile.
Hurled, would shatter at even this slight distance,
And he was so vast now, pinked and punctured in every limb
That the liquor could not fall at all amiss.
Not a drop would splash me.
Not a soul would care.

But then I nodded, and knowing it a terrible thing,
Smiled.
"I did come," I allowed, and set the bottle at a marble angel's feet,
"But not for you."
Then turning, flinched to find
The Knight, my Bravo, lance-length behind me,
Mounted, girded silver-bright, and watching,
As the waiting Quest of his Knight-brethren watched,
Silent beneath the Woodcutter's battleflag.

"Lady?" he said, and we both ignored
The Dragon's caustic snort.
He leaned him low across his horse's crest
Hand out, as though to swing me up before
And whisk me galloping away from the crude beast's insult.
I turned toward the gate
And managed not to laugh at either of us.

"I am weary," I told him,
And all the rest, before I walked away.


VII


Do not ask me how they killed him

I cannot tell you by what means they cut his thread,
Draught-poisoned, lance-spitted through the raging heart
Or bled quietly, inexorably dry.
I can only tell you that the mule, wise creature,
Had not wandered far afield,
And that at his bridle, awaiting my return,
Stood the Woodcutter King.

And oh, I had thought myself to cold for this,
My heart too scarred so to leap and flutter,
My stomach too soured for the sudden twist of hope,
My guilt-scarred face too stiff to crumple
Under that tearful, terrible regard.

"It is you," he said, when silence stretched too thin
And the ghosts of our breath crowded whisper-close,
"I had hoped you'd come."
And weeping, smiling, he strode to me,
His ironclad arms outstretched to gather me like cordwood to his breast,
As if he could shoulder me home singing to that long-lost valley springtime.
Oh, I had thought my heart broken already,
I truly had.

I pressed a claw-curled hand at his breastplate,
And, knowing it a terrible thing,
I bowed.
"I did come, Majesty," I said,
Waved my stick at the tumult below,
And prayed my voice, at least, would stay true,
"But I did not come for you."
And turning, would have fled,

188

Whipped that mule to frothing to escape the horrid
Welling softness I could feel,
Melting my spine from within, turning me to butter
And silly, bitter tears.

But I had not a Jack's luck, nor magical boots
Nor gold-saddled destrier,
Nor even, anymore, a Princess's dancing grace.
His hands were gentle as summer when my feet betrayed me,
And he swept me off the gravel road
And onto the cart-seat without a word.
"You mustn't," I managed,
Crow croaking, taut as wire when he swung up beside
And shook the mule's reins, slap flap along his back,
"Great King, I am not who you think-"

"No more am I," he said, and clucked his tongue
As the iron wheels crackled, coming about.
"For you think me a King, and a Hero of legend."

"And are you not?"  Easier now to cackle, hag-mad,
With my heart breaking in my ruined throat.
He flinched, a little, when I rapped the graven steel
(Three steeds, rampant athwart a mountain made of glass,)
Which spanned his breast with fame.

But he shook his head, and up the road he drove --
Away from the smoke and murder,
That clogged the guilt-grey valley,
Away from the bitter end
Beyond which I had never thought to look.
"I am not," he said, buckling the iron loose with a clang
That rattled winter crows, heckling from the trees.

"What I am, is a Father.
One who has sorely missed his daughter,
And would know her from ten thousand just alike."
And here, he loosed his hand from its sheltering steel,
Swept a grizzle of hair, once chestnut brown,
From his careworn face, and I could not help but see
The Woodcutter's son inside the coat of Kingly maille.
A man I had been too young to see,
When I had seen him last,
When I had shamed him last.

And I knew then, I would let him take me home –
Not to Court, or cavern,
But to the kindly, waiting Witch,
With her goose and her girl and her merry blue eye;
Where I might learn in peace what I needed now to know
But had not grasped from tutor or torment;
How to live, and heal, and read the future
In the ashes of the past:
How to meet my father's eye, in time,
Without the burn of shame:
How to love again the fit and feel
Of name and skin, scarred both alike.
And if he saw in me, betimes,
The ghost of his lost little girl and grieved,
Well.
Perhaps I could someday learn
To forgive her haunting golden shade.

## *About the Author*

Catt Kingsgrave has been writing fiction and verse since the early 1980's, and despite everything, she has not yet seen fit to desist. With works ranging from Urban- and Mythic Fantasy through Horror and Erotica, she has a decided taste for the Gothic and macabre, and takes delight in making all her works as difficult to classify as possible.

She lives with her partner of 28 years, and four cats in an upstate New York home that was built a century or so before the State in which she was born was made a part of the Union. When not writing, she has been known to indulge in random bouts of theatre, songwriting, dance, painting, home repair, volunteer rape crisis counseling, and folk music. Her interests are zombie outbreak preparedness, criminal profiling, gardening, and full-contact applied mythology.

She does not make jam.